Meeting
MR. WRIGHT

Meeting
MR. WRIGHT

A NOVEL BY
CASSIE CROSS

Chapter ONE

A year ago, if someone had told me that I would be spending a Friday night in an airport trying to pick up a guy, I would've laughed in their face.

A year ago I was still with Ethan.

Back then I would've thought that *I* would be getting married this weekend, not traveling across the country to my best friend Gabby's wedding. But Ethan had other plans, like fucking some random chick he met at happy hour on my 1,000 thread-count Egyptian cotton sheets. He thought I was working late. I came home early.

Surprise!

Ethan is the reason I don't work late anymore. He's also the reason I promised myself that I wouldn't fall in love again. I'd be crazy to open myself up to that kind of heartbreak again, right?

Staying out of the dating game is easy, but I would be lying if I said that I don't miss the scratch of Ethan's stubble on my face when he kissed me, or that I don't long for the feeling of his weight on top of me when we were in bed. I suppose that's why I'm at a bar in the middle of Dallas/Fort Worth International Airport, sipping on a cocktail and sitting next to the most gorgeous man I've ever seen.

We've been talking for half an hour, both of us waiting out a line of storms that have delayed every outbound plane in the area. I've booked a seat on a flight leaving first thing in the morning, and there's a room waiting for me in the hotel that's attached to the terminal. I should go up there and get some sleep, or finish one of the many projects that I have going on right now. But there's something about this man that makes me want to stay right where I am. Of course, it doesn't hurt that he's incredibly nice to look at.

I don't even know his name, but I like the velvety look of his close-cropped light brown hair and the sexy ruggedness of the couple of days' worth of stubble on his face. I like the cool depths of his bright blue eyes and the infectiousness of his smile. I want him, there's no doubt about it. I want to see him naked at some point this evening, but I'm completely unpracticed in the art of the one-night stand. I have no idea how to be even remotely sexy, but I'm flirting with him shamelessly. And he's flirting back.

"What happened here?" I ask, tracing the long, jagged scar that stretches out a few inches below his thumb. His skin feels electric beneath my fingers and when I touch him, he looks at me like he never wants me to stop. Unless my raging hormones are making me imagine that, which is entirely possible.

"This?" he asks, leaning in closer as he twists his wrist. "I was rappelling down the side of a cliff and my harness slipped. I reached out for leverage and cut myself."

"Rappelling?"

He grins. "Yeah, it's when you descend from a rock face using ropes and-"

"I know what rappelling is," I say, laughing. "I just thought that you were trying to impress me." I want to rappel *him*. Start at his head and work my way down, down, down.

"I am trying to impress you, but that's actually what happened." He looks down at what's left of the beer in his glass, and then he slides to his right a little, until his arm is touching mine. "What about you?"

"What about me?"

"Any impressive scars?" He smiles again, and its imperfection is endearing. His bottom lip is a little fuller than the top, and one of his front teeth is just the tiniest bit out of alignment with the rest. I'm pretty sure he knows how charming that smile is and the effect that it has on women. He's using it to his advantage tonight.

"Nothing really impressive, but I do have this," I tell him, pointing at my chin.

He slides his fingers along the underside of my jaw and tilts my head up so he can get a better look. The pad of his thumb grazes my scar, and I shiver. I hope he doesn't notice the way my breath catches when he touches me. I don't want to come off as desperate for him as I actually am.

"What's the story?"

"It's not even remotely cool as rappelling," I say. He looks at me expectantly. "I was at Girl Scout camp when I was, I don't know…seven maybe? It was my troop's turn to clean up the mess hall, and we were all running around and acting stupid. One of the girls started chasing me and I tripped, fell, and hit the edge of a bench."

He sucks in a breath through clenched teeth as he grimaces.

"Ouch. I guess you're not good in situations where fleeing is required?"

"I generally avoid situations where fleeing is required, actually. I'm small, so I guess I could always hope that someone would take pity on me and pick me up to expedite the fleeing process and limit the amount of damage I could do to myself while running." I'm talking way too much, but I just can't seem to help myself.

"I'd pick you up, but it wouldn't be out of pity." There's a mischievous look in his eyes that makes me want to wrap my body around his, and I'm beginning to get a sense that the two of us might have the same endgame in mind.

"So," he says, rubbing the palms of his hands on his jeans. "Are you going to tell me your name?"

For a split second I consider making one up, but even though he's a complete stranger, it feels wrong to want to lie to him.

"Callie. My name is Callie."

"Short for…" He draws out the 'r' as he searches for a name to guess. "Calliope?" He seems really proud of himself for thinking of another name, and it's disarmingly cute.

"Good guess," I tell him. "It's Callista. And your name is?"

"Nate."

"Short for…Michael?" It's an idiotic thing to say, but he laughs anyway.

"It's nice to meet you, Callie." My name sounds like heaven when he says it, and he takes my hand in his. His palm is a little rough, and I imagine what it would feel like sliding across the small of my back.

"It's nice to meet you, too," I say. For a very brief moment, I think about asking him where he's headed, but I decide against it. One-night stands aren't supposed to get invested, and I don't even want to know the slightest bit about his personal life, including where he's from or where he's going. I wish there was a way for me to turn off my mind and think with my vagina. Sex should be easy, but my brain has a way of complicating things.

"I was pissed when my flight got canceled, but now…" Nate says, looking down at our fingers which are loosely entwined. Somewhere in the back of my head I know that he's playing me, but I don't care. I just really don't care.

When he looks up, I catch his gaze, and we look at each other for a very long time. Butterflies circle my stomach, flapping their wings against my insides, and I feel like it might kill me to look away from him. It's been forever since someone has made me feel this way, and I want to keep feeling it. I'm trying to figure out a way to ask him upstairs to my room without sounding like I'm asking him upstairs to my room. I'm such a failure at casual sex.

Thankfully the bartender interrupts my frenzied thoughts when he walks over and asks if we'd like another round.

"No," I reply softly, still looking at Nate. His face falls with disappointment for just a split second before understanding lights his eyes.

He holds up has hand and shakes his head. The bartender walks away.

"Callie, I never do this, but-"

"I have a room," I say, interrupting him to keep him from finishing that sentence. Because 'I never do this' is the kind of thing that people who typically do this a lot tend to say. And I'm okay with that, really. But I don't want to hear it.

"Okay." Nate flashes a smile as he stands up and takes my hand, threading his fingers through mine. Then, he slings his duffel bag over his shoulder and leads me out of the bar.

We make our way through the crowded terminal to the hotel, looking at each other every few steps and grinning like a couple of fools.

The elevator can't come quickly enough.

I fumble with the key card in the lock, a mixture of nerves and excitement making my hands shake. As if Nate wants to see just how much of an effect he has on me, he wraps his arms around my waist, pulling me against him until I can feel every inch of his chest against my back. It takes me three tries to even get the damn card in the slot, and the longer it takes me, the more my hands shake.

"If you don't get this door unlocked, I'm going to break it down," he says, his voice a low rumble despite his teasing words. I take a deep breath to smooth over my jitters. "Let me help you," he says, gentle now as his lips brush across the shell of my ear. He doesn't seem to be nearly as nervous as I am, if he's even nervous at all. He unlocks the door with a sure, steady hand.

Once we're in the room, Nate tosses his bag to the side and pushes the door shut with his heel. Then he takes my face in his hands and kisses me like he can't get enough, like he's been waiting to do this his whole life. Our mouths melt together in long, slow kisses and then urgent, faster, needier ones. He brings my arms up and over his shoulders, clasping my hands together behind his neck.

"Hold onto me," he says. And I do.

Nate kisses me again, and all I can think about is the way he tastes, the way he feels. He slides his hands down the small of my back, down the backs of my thighs, and he lifts me up. I wrap my legs around his waist, anchoring myself to him, not caring about what's going to happen next as long as he keeps kissing me like he's never going to stop. He gently lowers me onto the bed, then pulls off my shoes, grinning at me as he playfully tosses them across the room. I help him by unbuttoning my jeans, then he tugs on the cuffs, sliding the denim down my thighs as I take off my shirt.

I lie back and enjoy the view as Nate pulls his shirt over his head and then unzips his pants. They fall to the floor, revealing a pair of boxes with yellow smiley faces all over them. I can't help but grin when I see them, and I trace the hem that hangs over his right thigh with my big toe.

"Are these your sexy shorts?" I ask.

He seems confused for a second, then catches on to what I'm asking after he looks down at what he's wearing.

"Hey," he replies, pretending to be offended. "I've gotten lots of compliments on these."

I don't even want to think about just how many compliments he's gotten on these boxers, so luckily he distracts me by sliding them down his hips. And my eyes are glued to him. His body is *insane.* Sturdy. Muscular. Perfect.

"C'mere," I say, crooking my finger at him, trying to be seductive and sexy and failing miserably. It doesn't matter, he doesn't seem to care.

Nate kneels over me on the bed, leaning down and kissing me before he reaches behind my back and unclasps my bra. He kisses my breasts, licking slow, torturous circles around my nipples that make my toes curl. My hands are everywhere, slipping across his broad shoulders and tight muscles, and I can't kiss him enough. His skin is salty and sweet. I love the little sounds that he makes when I press my lips here, touch him there, and gently slide my palm along the length of his erection. He sighs, resting his head in the crook of my neck.

"Do you like that?" I ask, wanting to be sure that I make this good for him.

"Yeah," he replies with a breathy laugh that warms my breast, and then his mouth finds its place on my skin. I continue sliding my hand up and down, and he bucks his hips against me as we kiss. When his breathing speeds up and his kisses become a little unfocused, he pulls away and kisses a trail down my stomach to the insides of my thighs. And then, oh. *Oh.*

"Oh my god," I sigh, and Nate lets out a little hum of a laugh that vibrates against me and makes my eyelids flutter shut. He works magic with his tongue and fingers as I sink back into the mattress and let myself drift. I drift and drift. Sometimes my eyes are closed and sometimes I look down at him while he's looking up at me and I have this crazy desire to run my fingers through his short hair. To scratch his scalp with my fingernails, because I think he'd like it.

So I do. And he likes it. And I like what he's doing to me so much that it isn't long until he makes me come in a warm, lapping wave that reaches out from my belly, cresting against my fingertips and toes.

Nate is obviously pleased with himself as I pull him up for a kiss, but it doesn't last as long as I'd like because his lips leave mine when he sits up and reaches for his jeans at the foot of the bed. He pulls a condom out of his back pocket, and I'm so glad he wants to be safe. It would be too easy for me to be stupid with him.

He kneels in front of me, my legs on either side of his as he looks down, his eyes locked with mine. I can't read his expression, can't tell exactly what he wants me to do next. And it's killing me, because whatever he wants me to do, I want to do it. One of his hands lightly traces the outside of my calf and the other cups my foot, lifting it until it rests on his shoulder. He turns his head and plants a sweet, gentle kiss on the inside of my ankle.

"You are so beautiful," he says, his voice very soft and very deep at the same time. I'm lying naked in front of him, so he knows this is a sure thing. He doesn't need to flatter me, but still…I'm flattered. What am I supposed to say? You're handsome? I'd like to lick every square inch of your body?

He doesn't wait for me to figure it out, he just leans down and kisses me as he hooks his arms under mine. I reach up and touch his face, wondering why all of this feels so tender when it isn't supposed to mean anything at all. Nate presses his forehead against mine as he slowly pushes into me. He sighs and runs his fingers through my hair, and somehow it feels like we've been together like this before. He knows every spot to touch that makes me gasp, every stretch of skin to slide his tongue across that opens me up to him. He brings me to the edge of pleasure and pulls me back, again and again, until my whole body is humming and desperate. When I finally fall, I bury my face in his neck. He follows soon after, peppering my face with kisses.

After, we lie there in bed, clinging to each other. Until a kiss turns into more kisses and a touch turns into a thousand more. Until he's inside me again and my body is wrapped around his and our names fall from each other's lips. We follow the same pattern all night, over and over again, until we finally drift off to sleep.

I wake up just before dawn, wrapped in Nate's arms. I've never been so comfortable and so scared in my entire life. I don't want to walk out of this room and never see him again, but more than that I don't want him to become another Ethan. I'm scared he'll break what's left of my heart, and I'll get so hardened against men that I won't be able to have another night like this again.

No, it's better for me to leave things as they are and let this night become a memory.

I get dressed quietly and gather my things, ignoring the nagging ache I feel as I slip out the door.

Chapter TWO

*G*abby and I sit side-by-side in the bed of her fiancée Ben's old pickup truck. We're parked on the top of a hill at the edge of the property that Mr. and Mrs. Wright, Ben's parents, have owned for the past twenty years. The view is so lush and green and beautiful that I want to spend the rest of my trip right in this spot. It's still really early—the sun is just beginning to rise—and the two of us are huddled under a thick blanket, thermoses full of hot chocolate warming our hands.

"What's over there?" I ask, pointing at an incredibly large area of land about 50 yards away that's cordoned off with bright yellow caution tape.

"That's where the tent for the reception is going to go. Amy blocked it off so that no one would drive on it and get tire tracks in the grass. She said she didn't want the pictures to look 'rednecky,'" Gabby replies.

Amy, Ben's mother, is quite possibly one of the best event planners that I've ever met. Not that I've met all that many, mind you, but she's pretty great at it is what I'm saying. She also happens to be an incredibly sweet woman and she treats Gabby like one of her own children. That puts her up pretty high in my book.

"In a place like this, I don't think the pictures could be anything but gorgeous." I take a deep breath as I look up at the stunning purples and pinks in the sky. The sun starts to peek over the horizon.

"You really like it here, don't you?"

"I do. I'm glad you had the sense to take off the week before your wedding and invite me along. It's a nice little vacation."

"That was part of my wedding requirements checklist, actually." Gabby unscrews the top of her thermos and pours some hot chocolate into two small styrofoam cups. She hands one to me and keeps the other. "Beautiful locale, nice weather, good vacation spot for Callie."

"And it's free," I say, laughing.

"Yes, free is good. We definitely lucked out with that."

"When is everyone else getting here?"

"Thursday," she says, bringing her cup to her lips. Tendrils of steam curl into the air around her fingers.

We both look out over the mountains, watching the day come to life. I decide that this might be the right time to tell Gabby about what happened with Nate. As it is she'll probably want to kill me for not telling her the second that I stepped off the plane yesterday morning. But Ben was there with her, and then the three of us spent the day driving through the mountains. This is the first one-on-one time that we've had together since I got here.

"So," I say, fiddling with the edge of the blanket. "I did something on Friday night."

Gabby's expression changes ever so slightly, from content to cautious.

"If I have to find a new maid of honor, Callie, I swear I'll-"

"What, do you think I committed a felony or something?" I ask, laughing.

Gabby laughs too, and I can't help but think about what a lovely bride she'll be. She has flawless mocha-colored skin and shiny, gorgeous hair that comes down to her shoulders in springy, tight spirals. She's radiant even in the barely there early morning light.

"*Did* you commit a felony?"

"Not this time."

"Good," she replies. "It would've been difficult to find someone who could fit into that tiny dress of yours on such short notice anyway."

"We have six more days to focus on the wedding, Gabs," I say, trying to sound exasperated. "Can we please just focus on *me* right now?"

Gabby bumps my shoulder with hers. "What is it?"

I twist my fingers together, nervous to tell her about this for some reason. But she's my best friend. If I can't tell her, who can I tell?

"I, um…I slept with a guy I met at the airport." I can't help but cringe as I say it. It's not that I'm ashamed or anything…it's just that the words sound wrong coming out of my mouth for some reason. Like I'm telling her about something someone else did.

"Is that why you didn't come until yesterday morning?" she asks, her eyes wide.

"I came Friday night, actually. Several times."

Gabby leans forward, clutching her stomach as she laughs. "Oh my god, Callie."

"Seriously though, there was actually a weather delay. That was how I spent it."

"I thought you were swearing off men?" she asks. It's not an accusatory tone, but more of an I-told-you-so. Because she doesn't think that I can do it, doesn't think that I'll stick with it.

"I swore off love, not men," I remind her. "I don't need Ethan: Part Two."

"Was it good?"

I take a deep breath and stretch out my arms, sinking back against the cab of the truck. "It was better than good. It was…amazing." I know that's not the right word to describe it, but I can't think of another one that will do it justice. Maybe there isn't a word that will do it justice.

"Who was it?"

"Just some guy I met," I tell her.

"So you just said goodbye and that was that?"

I can tell that Gabby is having difficulty grasping the fact that I've done something like this. Truthfully, that it stuns her makes me proud in an odd sort of way. It makes me feel less predictable, like maybe I'm not as boring as I think I am, not boring enough to push Ethan to look for entertainment elsewhere.

"I actually didn't say goodbye to him," I admit. "I kind of left while he was sleeping."

"That is *so* not like you," she says. She almost sounds proud.

"I know." I don't tell her that I regret leaving the way that I did, that I wish I had gotten his number. No good can come from that admission. "I'm just moving on, I guess." That part is true.

"Really?" She takes a sip of her hot chocolate. "In that case, I need to tell you something, too."

I know by the tone of her voice that this 'something' is going to be a thing that I don't want to hear. She says the words slowly and deliberately, like she's defusing a bomb.

"Doesn't the sky look like a watercolor?" I look up, mainly to avoid Gabby's gaze. I'm an expert avoider.

"Callie."

"You know, I've been thinking. Maybe I should move out here. I like the country, and it's as pretty as Texas but more temperate. It doesn't feel like we've walked through the gates of Hell when we step outside here."

"Callie," Gabby says again, still sounding so patient. She lets me work through things in my own way, in my own time. It's one of the things that I love most about her.

I stop talking and stare straight ahead. I prefer not to look at the bullet when it's coming straight at me. I'm pretty sure I know what this one is anyway.

"He's bringing someone."

Despite my efforts to avoid it, it hits me right in the chest. In the heart. But the thing is, I thought the words would hurt more than they do. They sting, it's true, but it's not the gut-wrenching pain I was expecting. Still, I sigh, looking to my right across the hilltops, hating myself for telling Gabby and Ben that I wouldn't mind if they invited Ethan to the wedding. Ethan and Ben have known each other for years, though. How could I have said no?

"It's not *her* is it?" I'm not sure I could handle him bringing the girl he cheated on me with. I would be surprised if Ethan did something that tacky, but I never thought he'd cheat on me, either.

"No, it's someone else. Someone new."

That makes me feel marginally better, despite the fact that he's obviously moving on quickly. "Okay."

"I'm sorry," Gabby says, her eyes full of sadness. "I shouldn't have invited him."

"It's okay," I say, smiling. And it is okay. "He's Ben's best friend. Him not being invited would be like me not being invited, which would be completely unacceptable."

Gabby smiles, and I decide then and there not to let Ethan's presence bother me. For her sake.

"When's he coming?" I ask.

"Tonight. I don't think he plans on hanging out with us very much. He wanted to bring someone with him so he wouldn't be-"

"I don't need to know." I sigh and hold up my thermos. "Why didn't you bring something to spike this with? I'm going to need something a lot stronger than hot chocolate if I'm going to make it through the next week."

"Oh, I think you'll be all right," she replies playfully. "I've got something planned for you to take your mind off things."

I can see the mischievous glint in her eyes, and I know better than to ask her what's coming. Besides, it's much too beautiful of a morning for me to worry about it anyway. The sun is bright, burning off what's left of the morning fog. I close my eyes, loving the warmth on my face and the sounds of the birds chirping around us. I haven't felt this peaceful in a long time.

Gabby and I somehow manage to drift off to sleep, and we wake up close to ten. She seems a bit frantic as we both climb out of the truck bed and into the cab. She speeds along the dirt paths leading back to the house, and I get the impression from the look on her face that she hasn't told Ben's parents exactly where we were and what we were doing this morning.

I'm kind of impressed by the way Gabby's driving Ben's truck; she maneuvers the thing like she's lived on this land her whole life. When the main house comes into view, I see Mrs. Wright sitting on the porch steps, waiting for us like a true mother.

"You're in trouble," I tease, but Gabby isn't in the mood for it. The brakes squeal as we come to a stop.

"Where have you girls been?" Mrs. Wright says as she rushes over to us. She cups Gabby's face in her hands, looking relieved to see her. "What would I tell Ben if his bride went missing right before the wedding?"

"We're fine Amy," Gabby says, smiling through her embarrassment.

"Sorry we worried you, Mrs. Wright," I say.

Ben's mom is a short, slightly round woman, with reddish brown hair and the brightest blue eyes I've ever seen. Everything about her is so warm and friendly that it's nearly impossible not to smile and feel right at home around her, even when she's being a total mother bear.

"Call me Amy," she says, smiling.

"Leave them alone, Mom," a strangely familiar voice calls from the porch. "I'm here for all your motherly nagging needs. Gab's getting married in a few days, she needs to de-stress."

When I look up, I see the very last person I ever expected to see here standing on the front porch. Hell, he's the very last person I expected to see anywhere again. Ever.

It's Nate.

Airport Nate.

Best-sex-of-my-life Nate.

Guy-I-left-naked-in-bed-without-saying-goodbye Nate.

He's just as gorgeous as I remember. I want to run toward him *and* I want to run in the opposite direction. Instead of doing either, I'm frozen in my spot. Either he doesn't get a good look at my face right away, or he doesn't recognize me. I'm not sure which option I would prefer. I'm hiding on the passenger side of the truck, trying to buy some time.

"All right then, smartass," Amy says. "You want to be nagged? Clean your room. Do your homework. Wash your face. Wash your hands."

"Mow the lawn," he shouts with a laugh, the most gorgeous smile on his face.

"Rake the leaves!"

"Is that it?"

"I've got more," Amy replies. "Remember your manners. Give your future sister-in-law a hug, and say hello to Callie."

Nate pauses a second when he hears my name, but he makes his way down the stairs anyway, and I'm still trying to figure out what to do. I'm going to have to step out and say hello to him eventually. As if Amy can sense my discomfort, she walks over and grabs my hand, pulling me around the front of the truck towards certain embarrassment.

"Don't be shy," she says. My eyes meet Nate's as he's hugging Gabby.

He lets her go, and I know he's a little dumbfounded that I'm here. The corners of his eyes crinkle as he squints, like he's trying to make sure I'm really standing in front of him. But then he smiles, like he's relieved. And the beauty in it is unnerving.

"Nate," Gabby says, then looks in my direction. "This is my best friend Callie. Callie, this is Nate."

I'm silently begging him not to let on that we've already met. I don't want to explain that to Gabby right now, and I really don't want to explain that to his mother.

"Callie," he says warmly, familiarly, as he reaches out and takes my hand. "It's nice to meet you."

Chapter
THREE

*N*ate and I are just standing here, hands clasped together, smiling at each other like idiots. The second my hand slipped into his, all my nervousness fell away. And now all I can think about is the fact that he's touching me, and that makes me remember the way he touched me two nights ago, which makes me want him to touch me again. Everywhere. It's not until Gabby coughs that my eyes even lift to his, and I can feel my cheeks flush. I had completely forgotten that there are other people standing here with us.

And then I see Nate's mother, who is smiling too, and I remember that it's her son that I'm standing here lusting after, and my cheeks feel hotter. Nate grins at me like he knows what I'm thinking.

I let go of his hand like it's on fire. But it's too late, because Gabby's already seen that there's something between Nate and me, and even though she doesn't know exactly what that thing is, I can tell that she's plotting already and I'm going to have to find a way to put a stop to that.

"You two seem to have hit it off," Amy says in a singsongy voice with a knowing smile.

I want the ground to open up and swallow me whole. Immediately, if not sooner.

Thankfully Gabby recognizes the horrified look on my face and she steps in to steer the conversation away from me.

"When did you get in?" she asks Nate. "I thought you weren't coming until tomorrow."

Nate looks over at me before he answers. "Dad sent me a text to tell me that he and Ben are camping tonight. I wanted to go, so I took a train from DC."

"Is that where you live?" The question comes out before I can stop my stupid mouth from moving.

Nate grins. "No, I live in Colorado. I just made a detour before I came here. I went to visit a friend."

"Where's Ben?" Gabby asks.

"He's fishing with his father, trying to catch something for dinner tonight. We'll probably wind up having hot dogs," Amy says, grinning as she makes her way back to the house. She opens the screen door and turns around. "Nate, will you come help me bring the card tables down from the attic?"

Nate nods, then looks at Gabby. "It's good to see you," he says before turning to me. He takes my hand again, and I can't even think straight, not while he's touching me. "Callie, it was very nice to meet you." He winks at me before he turns and walks up the steps, stopping once at the door to smile at me again.

Gabby looks at me with wide eyes as she grabs my arm and leads me to a bench a few feet away where we can talk without worrying about anyone overhearing us.

"What. Was. That?" she asks. "I was hoping you two would hit it off, but I never thought…"

I'm not really sure what to do now. I know I should tell her, because she's my best friend and I've never kept anything from her. I don't think I *could* keep this from her, even if I tried. It's bound to come out at some point, and at least if I let her know now I can be the one who's in control of it. But once I tell her about my history with Nate, I know she'll start waxing philosophic about fate or something equally ridiculous. Gabby's such a hopeless romantic, bless her.

I might as well get this over with.

"Nate's the guy," I tell her. "The one from the airport."

"Are you kidding me?" She's so excited that I'm a bit worried that she's going to hyperventilate. "What are the odds of that? Holy shit."

"I bet they're pretty long," I tell her. Seriously long. "But I know that look on your face, and it's not-"

"It's fate," she says, clasping my hands in hers. "How can you think it's anything but fate, Callie?"

"I can think it's a coincidence, Gab. Because that's what it is." It's a delightful, scary coincidence.

"He likes you." She's not going to give up very easily.

"Stop it."

"Maybe one day-"

"No," I say firmly. I don't want her getting any more ideas or thinking that she can just bulldoze through my plans with her iron will. "You know I don't want that."

She rolls her eyes, but I shoot her a death glare that lets her know that I'm not kidding.

"He's the best man and you're the maid of honor. I paired the two of you up at the bridal party's table and everything."

I sigh. "As long as that's all the pairing up you do, that's fine."

"It might be out of my hands. He's super charming," she says slyly, looking at me out of the corner of her eye. She's always doubted my commitment to my new life goal of never having my heart smashed again by someone I stupidly fall in love with. I wonder what it'll take to get her to believe that I'm serious.

"I think I'm aware of how charming he is," I tell her. I mean, the man charmed my pants right off. "How come I haven't met him before? I don't even remember ever hearing about him."

"You knew Ben had a brother," she says in a not-so-subtle chastising tone.

"I knew he had a brother, but I didn't know he was hot." I didn't know he was *Nate*.

Gabby rolls her eyes. "When was I supposed to tell you that? When you were dating Ethan or when you were swearing off men?"

"Swearing off *love*," I correct her. She has a point though, I don't try to argue that.

"Oh, excuse me," she says, smiling. "He lives in Boulder and manages a chain of sporting goods stores, in case you wanted to know."

"I didn't," I say, even though that's a tiny white lie. I shouldn't want to know, that's the real issue here.

"The way he looked at you, Callie," she says dreamily, and I can tell that I'm not going to like where that train of thought is heading.

"Can we please stop talking about this now?"

"If we stop talking about this, I'm dragging you to the garage to help me make centerpieces."

Arts and crafts time sounds like paradise compared to twenty questions. I stand and brush off my pants.

"All right, let's go."

Three hours and thirty centerpieces later, I'm sitting on the front porch sipping an iced tea that Amy made especially for me. My right hand is throbbing, because apparently I'm not cut out to make centerpieces and my fingers swell after an afternoon of light manual labor. If I never see another bow again it'll be too soon. I was intrigued when Gabby first told me about her plans for a small wedding on Ben's family's farm in Virginia, but I find myself wishing that she had gone even smaller. Like a courthouse in Dallas kind of small. Then I wouldn't be dealing with centerpieces and swollen fingers. And I wouldn't be worrying about what's going to happen with Nate.

I can understand what drew her to this place, though. The land is gorgeous, and the house, it's absolutely breathtaking. Somehow both large and quaint at the same time, the Wright home is hugged by a wide wraparound porch. Brightly colored azaleas line the perimeter, popping against the white siding. There's a smaller guest house down a short path connected to the back of the main one, which is where I'm staying along with the rest of the wedding party, whenever they arrive. The guest house is nicer than the one I grew up in. I'm admiring the cozy looking patio attached to it when the screen door behind me opens with a high-pitched squeak. The wood planks along the length of the porch creak as someone walks toward me. Every nerve in my body comes alive before I even turn around. My body knows who it is before my mind can even process it.

"Mind if I sit?" Nate asks.

I look up at him, squinting against the glare of the sun. "No, I don't mind," I reply, shaking my head.

He sits down next to me, stretching his long legs out in front of him, and he's quiet for a few moments, fiddling with a string that dangles from the frayed hem of his khaki shorts. As I watch his fingers, I wish there was some way to get rid of this light nervous feeling I have in my stomach.

"So," Nate says. "I have to admit that you were a first for me. I've never been so bad in bed that a woman felt the need to leave before the sun even came up."

Regret fills my chest, making its way up my throat, and I have to swallow it down. Nate must understand the look on my face, because he bumps his leg against mine to let me know that he's just kidding, even though I'm sure he would like an answer as to why I abandoned him while he was still naked and wrapped up in the sheets on the bed in my hotel room.

"I think you know you were anything but bad," I say. I can't help but smile at him, like I don't have any control over what my body does when he's around me.

"But you wanted to leave."

"I *had* to leave," I clarify. "I'm sorry that I did it the way that I did, but I went to the airport that day to catch a flight here, not…to do that. I was totally not expecting it. Even after I did it, strange as that sounds."

He studies my face, and I don't like the way his eyes seem to cut right through me, down the parts that I don't want anyone to see. "It's okay," he finally says, and I get the sense that it really is.

"I don't date," I blurt out. I immediately regret saying it, because while it's the truth, it makes it seem like I think he wants more from me when all we shared was some meaningless sex. A one-night stand. "I mean, I wasn't sure how to say goodbye to you, so I figured it would be best to go while you were sleeping. I just…I haven't done anything like that before."

"So you said." Nate's grinning, and he's seemingly beyond expecting an explanation. He's just enjoying watching me tie myself into knots while trying to rationalize my behavior.

"I'm sorry, I'm bungling this," I tell him, frustratedly running my fingers through my hair.

"So what you're telling me is that you used me for my body?"

"It's such a nice body." The words slip out before I can even stop myself from saying them, and I know, I just *know* my mouth is going to get me into some big trouble around this man.

Nate laughs again; it's a deep, genuine laugh and his eyes are so bright when they look into mine. "You're welcome to it anytime."

Even though he's just teasing me, I know he means what he said. My cheeks grow hot, and I accidentally knock over my glass. Tea seeps across the bottom step, and I bend down to pick it up at the same time Nate does. Our heads bump together and Nate presses his palm against my forehead at the same time I do, and we're sitting there with our fingers kind of entwined against my head. The situation is so weird that I'm fairly certain it's a concussion-related hallucination.

"Are you okay?" Nate asks, concern in his voice. "Do you want me to get my dad to check you out? He's a doctor and-"

I stand up, not completely steady on my feet. But that isn't because of my head.

"No, I'm okay. You? That's good. I, uh…" I point somewhere behind me. "I better go. I was just gonna…do some stuff. There's lots of stuff to do. Over there. In my room."

There's an adorably crooked smile on Nate's face, and he must be trying really hard not to laugh at me because he has to know that we didn't hit our heads hard enough for me to be acting like this. His words did a number on me. His damn flirty, sexy, knock-me-off-my-feet words.

"I'll see you later? Maybe tomorrow, or sometime after today. Just not now. Later. Bye," I say, watching my feet as they make their way down the stone path. I'm too embarrassed to look back at him. He's got to be laughing at me by now. If he isn't there's something wrong with him.

"Callie?"

"Yeah?" I turn, and there's that crooked grin. Why does he have to be so gorgeous? Why do I have to be such an idiot?

He points in the opposite direction. "The guest house is that way."

Sure enough, he's right. I mean, he would be right, wouldn't he? He grew up here. And…god, I just want to die. What is it about him that twists me into knots and makes me act like a complete moron? I really wish there was some way I could make myself disappear.

I give Nate a small, shy wave before I go running towards the safety of the guest house, far away from him.

*L*ater that evening I'm standing in front of the mirror in my room, applying a coat of mascara. After I slide the wand back into the tube, I take a step back and give myself a once-over. At home, I usually wear my long blonde hair in a ponytail, but there isn't any humidity here in the early fall air, so I wear it down, tumbling over my shoulders. The navy blue dress I'm wearing looks good against my skin and makes my eyes pop. I feel pretty for the first time in a while.

I can hear everyone laughing outside the window, can smell the smoke from the barbecue, and I'm impatient to go out there and join in on the fun. I dab some gloss on my lips before I turn and leave. When I open the door, I see a small cooler at my feet. I bend down and open the lid; it's full of ice. I'm a little confused, but then I see that there's a large basket just to the right of the cooler. Inside the basket is an ice pack, a bottle of ibuprofen and a pink helmet.

A laugh escapes my lips as I kneel down and read the small card that's tied to the basket's handle. I smile when I see what I'm certain is Nate's messy handwriting.

You definitely suck at fleeing.

Chapter FOUR

*A*s if it's not enough of a nightmare having Ethan in attendance at this wedding, somehow, because somebody somewhere hates me, he and his girlfriend *du jour* end up in the guest room right next to mine. Thankfully I haven't heard the headboard banging against my wall, but at the moment the two of them are milling around in the hallway right outside of our rooms. I'm watching them through the small crack in the door like a true stalker, waiting for them to leave so I can go outside and catch up with Gabby, Ben and Nate. We're supposed to be going down to the river, but Ethan and his lady friend are keeping me from dipping my toes in the water, which is annoying. I could just grow up and walk out there, but I'm not ready for all that yet.

Ethan is still very tall and very slim, still handsome in that bookish, nerdy kind of way that I always liked about him. He's wearing new glasses and his dark brown hair is longer than it used to be, the way I always liked it. It's curling just over his brow, and I used to love the way he'd push it back when he was reading, concentrating really hard. In college, I used to study his face almost as much as I studied my books.

Much as I hate to admit it, he looks good. I was hoping he'd show signs of being wrecked by the realization that I'm no longer in his life, but that appears to be a lost cause. It was probably a lost cause the moment I found him fucking that woman in our bed, but my heart is slowly catching up to my head. I'm making progress.

The girl he brought here as his date, Emily, is the complete opposite of me. She's tan with long, dark brown curly hair that's gorgeous and thick, and I kind of hate her for that. God, she's tall. Ethan used to tell me that he loved my height, loved tucking me under his arm, but seeing him laughing and wrapping his arm around that giraffe of a woman is making me feel like that's just another lie he told me, the asshole. I want to yank the door open and start yelling at him, but I don't do it, because I'm really trying to be less bitter about our breakup.

Finally the two of them make their way downstairs and I poke my head out into the hallway to make sure that the coast is clear. I can hear Emily's throaty laughter disappear outside after they shut the front door. I walk over to my window and watch them walk past Gabby, Ben and Nate. I'm such a creeper. And of course Gabby catches me looking. She glares at me, and instantly I know that I've got some public embarrassment coming my way.

"Get your ass down here, Callie." She yells so loudly that I'm sure even the people in the main house can hear her. I want to flip her off, but I manage to restrain myself. By the time I make my way out of the house, Ethan and Emily are halfway down the trail that leads to the river.

I get a good look at Ben and Nate standing next to each other, and if I didn't know that they were brothers, then I never would've guessed it at first glance. They're both tall, but that's about the only similarity they have to one another. Ben is a beanpole and Nate's built like a brick wall. Ben's hair is dark brown and curly, Nate's is a nearly brown dark blonde that's cropped short. Ben has a long face and a sharp nose, and Nate's face is angular, with a jawline most people would kill for.

Because Nate, Ben and Gabby are preoccupied talking about something or other, it takes them a minute to realize that I'm standing here waiting.

"Nice of you to finally show up," Ben says.

"Hey," I reply, pointing in the direction of his best friend who's about 50 yards away, reminding Ben that he played a small part in my tardiness by inviting Ethan here in the first place. "You don't get to say anything about that."

Ben, good guy that he is, has the decency to look contrite. "Sorry, Cal."

"You need to find some new friends." I smile to hide the honesty in my words, then look over at Nate, who's watching me intently. He's probably wondering what that exchange was all about, assuming Ben and/or Gabby haven't already told him the long story of how my heart was broken by the man I once thought of as the love of my life.

"Hi," Nate says, offering me a gentle grin.

"Hi." I grin back, wishing he wasn't so damn cute. Everything that I found charming about him in the airport that night is so amplified here. Maybe because I know I should stay away from him. Maybe because I know that I can't stay away from him while I'm here.

We all start walking and I gravitate toward Gabby, needing some kind of buffer between me and Nate.

"Are you still okay with Ethan being here?" she asks.

"Yes," I reply, and I mean it. Ethan being around is something that I'm going to have to get used to. Gabby's going to be Ben's wife soon, and Ethan is going to be a part of her life for as long as he's still friends with her husband. I don't want to make this situation awkward for anyone, most of all Gabby. It's been six months since Ben and I broke up. I need to get over it.

"Crap," Gabby says dramatically. "I forgot my sunscreen."

"I have some," I tell her, digging for the bottle I have stashed in my bag.

"No, I bought some especially for this trip to make sure I didn't get any tan lines. I can't have that in my wedding pictures." I love Gabby to death, I really do, but she's a horrible liar. "I need to go back to the house. Ben," she says, grabbing his hand. "Come with me."

Ben doesn't really seem down with this plan, but the last thing he's going to do is get on his fiancée's bad side a few days before his wedding. So he goes along with her scheme. Because that's what this is, I'm sure of it. A scheme. Based on the look on Nate's face, he knows it too.

"I guess we'll meet you down there," Ben says, looking innocently over at us as Gabby pulls him toward the house.

Nate looks over at me. "You know Gabby's trying to set us up, right?"

"Yeah," I tell him. "She's a horrible actress."

"That's a nice way of putting it."

"She's determined to get me on a date."

"I doubt you have trouble with that," he says, looking at me so intensely that I can feel the blush creeping up my cheeks. That seems to happen often whenever I'm around him.

"I meant that she's determined to get me to go out on a date, not to help me find one." I'm flattered anyway, which I suppose is what he was going for.

"So, yesterday when you said that you don't date-"

"I meant that I *really* don't date."

I can tell that Nate wants to ask me why, wants to find out more about that particular promise that I've made to myself, but he knows this isn't the time and it definitely isn't the place.

"Phew," he says, playfully wiping his forehead with the back of his hand. "I thought maybe it was me, that you were trying to let me down easy."

I laugh. "It's not you, trust me."

"Well." Nate shrugs as he looks down the dirt path sprawling in front of us. "How do you feel about a strictly platonic trip to the river? Because my brother and his bride aren't coming back."

I take a few steps forward, and soon we're walking side-by-side.

"I think I can handle a strictly platonic trip to the river."

*N*ate jostles open the rickety old door to the family's boathouse, and I keep a safe distance on a small patch of grass a few feet away, close to the river. The place looks ancient, and even though it's probably safe, it doesn't look all that safe to me.

"I'm just going to stay over here," I say, folding my arms across my chest.

"Nothing in here is going to get you." Nate seems amused by my reluctance to believe there isn't an axe-wielding murderer hanging out in there.

"I'm going to stay over here." I repeat. "And don't think about playing some trick on me to get me to go in there. I've seen enough movies to know what kinds of scary things happen in dark boathouses."

Nate shakes his head and laughs as he walks inside. "Would you leave me here?" he yells from inside. "If something scary happened inside this dark boathouse?"

"I don't know, maybe." I reach into my bag and pull out my sunscreen, then rub it on my shoulders and arms before the sun has a chance to burn me lobster red. When I'm finished applying the sunscreen, Nate walks out, his arms full.

"What are those?"

"These are inner tubes," he says slowly.

"I know what they are, but I want to know what you're doing with them."

"We're going to use them as floating apparatuses. You see, that's what they're for."

"No way," I say, looking at the water. "I thought we were just going to sit on the shore and, like, sun ourselves."

"Well, there isn't much shore to speak of, in case you didn't notice."

"I can set myself up on the grass, I don't have a problem with that."

"What kind of fun would that be?" he asks as he tosses the tubes onto the ground.

"The kind of fun that keeps me stationary and on dry land. Because I have the kind of luck where I'd float off down a tributary or whatever and wind up in the Atlantic."

Nate grins as he wraps his fingers around the hem of his shirt and lifts it over his head. When my eyes come to rest on the broad, tanned planes of his chest, I forget what I was even talking about. I'm preoccupied with maybe eventually putting my mouth on his body. Again. And again.

"Are you afraid of water, Callie?"

I shake my head to bring myself back into the moment, because I really don't need to be thinking about how good he looks with his shirt off, even though he looks really, *really* good.

"What?"

Nate laughs. "Are you afraid of water?"

"I'm not so much afraid of water as I just don't get into large bodies of it. Generally speaking."

"I'll tell you what," he says, undoing a knot in the rope that's wrapped around one of the inner tubes. "I'll tie your raft to mine and I'll keep us going in the right direction. If you drift off and float down a tributary or whatever into the Atlantic, I'll be right there with you."

I look at him skeptically. "You don't seem all that worried about our possible castaway status."

"Well, Ben and Gabby's wedding is in a few days and I would do pretty much anything to avoid having to wear a suit." He winks at me, and I swear my knees almost give out. Damn him.

I want to tell him that I think he'd look really good in a suit, but I refrain. That would only encourage him, and the last thing he needs is encouragement. "Okay," I say. "But I'll be keeping my eye on you."

"I'm looking forward to it." He tosses the tubes in the river, then steps in and turns toward me. "C'mon," he says, holding out his hand to help me into the water. "Just lean back and relax. I'll take care of the rest."

I haven't been in the water very long before I realize that floating to the Atlantic on this inner tube might not be such an awful thing after all. I love the sound of the water lapping against the rubber, the gentle rustling of the leaves as the breeze runs through them. The tips of my toes skim the surface of the water, and I kick a little over onto Nate.

He grins as he looks over at me. "You don't want to start something that you can't finish," he says, a wicked gleam in his eyes.

I start to flick some more water onto him when I hear a familiar throaty laugh. I sit up, balancing myself on the giant floating donut I'm draped over, and sure enough, Ethan and Emily are sitting together on the river bank across from us. Ethan is leaning over, looking like he's going in for a kiss. I groan quietly.

"What's the matter?" Nate asks, turning to see what I'm looking at.

I think I hear a soft 'oh' come from his direction, but I'm not sure.

"It's nothing," I reply as I lean back, trying to ignore them.

Nate's quiet for a few seconds before he says, "He's a dick for what he did to you."

I look over at him, not really surprised that he knows about me and Ethan, but I am kind of surprised that he said something about it. "Gabby told you?"

"My brother did, actually. He told me about what Ethan did and that his ex was coming, too. Gabby told me that the ex was you, and that you didn't want to make anyone uncomfortable this weekend, so to make sure that I didn't say anything about it. Not that it would've been hard to figure out that there's a history between the two of you, given the way that you look at him."

I'm surprised to hear that my face gives so much away; I thought I'd learned how to sufficiently school my expression when it comes to Ethan. "How do I look at him?"

"Like you want to rip his heart out of his chest."

"Then who thought it would be a good idea to put him and his new girlfriend in the room right next to mine?" I ask.

He sits up, and the water sloshes around him. "Shit, seriously?"

I laugh. "Yes, seriously."

"Do you want to move? You shouldn't have to deal with all that. We can find another room for you; there are plenty. I'll help you with your things."

It's nice that he's so concerned for me, and I'm glad that in addition to being so incredibly hot and so incredibly great in bed that he also seems to be a good person. I don't allow myself to think too much about it; seeming and being are two different things. I've been fooled by appearances before. The man on the other side of the shore is proof of that.

"I can stay where I am, it's okay," I reply, pulling my hair back into a ponytail. "I don't want to be petty about it."

Nate gives me a long look before he speaks again. "If you feel uncomfortable, you'll tell me?"

I feel a tingling warmth beneath my skin when he says those words. "I will."

"I'll kick his ass if you want me to."

Nate's so at ease out here, his left arm folded behind his head, the rope to my inner tube loosely grasped in his right hand. His legs are so long that they're knee-deep in the water, creating a nice drag that keeps us moving down the river at a very slow, leisurely pace.

"That's a sweet offer," I reply. "But I'd appreciate it if you just keep us steady on our course here."

He lets out a laugh through a wide, lazy smile. "You're really not into the outdoors, are you?"

"I'm more of a fan of air conditioning. And I like looking at nature, just not really participating in it."

"Have you ever been to Colorado?"

I shake my head. "Nope."

"You'd change your mind if you came to Boulder. It's gorgeous; you can't help but want to be outside all the time."

I want to tell him that if he knew me better he'd rethink that statement. I could help it, and I would help it. But he looks so happy that I decide to ask him a little bit about himself instead.

"Gabby told me that you manage a sporting goods store there, is that right?"

"I manage a chain of them, yeah. I worked there while I was in college, and when I graduated a few years ago they promoted me to store manager. Now I'm regional manager."

"That kind of job seems like it would suit you."

"It does?"

I nod. "Well, you rappel, as we both know. And you're an expert inner tube navigator." He smiles, and it seems to make him happy that I remember how he got that scar on his hand. How could I forget? Asking about that scar in the airport bar led to one of the best nights of my life.

"I take it your job keeps you in the air conditioning?"

"It does, as a matter of fact. I own my own business."

"Really?" Nate raises his eyebrows, and I get the feeling he's impressed with me.

"Really."

"A business that specializes in businessing, or..."

"I'm a web developer. I make websites for small businesses and charities. Things like that."

"Wow," he replies, raising his eyebrows. "That must be nice."

"I like being my own boss. I get to set my own hours, which is pretty great."

"There's a 'but' in there, I can tell."

I bite my bottom lip, dragging it through my teeth as I think of a way to address that 'but' without sounding like I'm ungrateful or unhappy. "I'm proud of the work that I do. But...sometimes it just feels so insignificant. When I was younger, I always thought that when I got out of college and started doing my own thing that I'd be making a real difference. That I'd be changing the world."

"We can't all cure cancer," he says, skimming his fingertips along the surface of the water. "Besides, I think scale is overrated when you talk about change. Just because it isn't big doesn't mean that you're not doing it."

"What do you mean?"

He shrugs. "Maybe you *are* changing the world."

"Doubtful," I reply. "None of my clients have ever said, 'Wow, Callie. That's a groundbreaking font choice."

Nate laughs and kicks his legs out of the water, sending a shower of droplets raining down in front of us.

"Maybe not, but you make a website for a business, and that increases their exposure, helps them generate sales and revenue. One of those business owners might take that money and help build a community center or start an outreach program. Or maybe they're taking the money that website helped them earn and sending their kid to college. Maybe that kid will do something great, and you'll have had a hand in it. You just have to look at things a little differently."

I turn to him, absolutely speechless, completely in awe. I haven't ever thought of it like that before. And even though I don't dare tell him this, a small part of me is beginning to look at *him* differently, too.

Nate and I continue floating along the river for a little while longer, the two of us silent more often than not, just enjoying each other's company and the beauty of the nature surrounding us. Soon, clouds roll in, and small droplets of rain plink against the water. Nate paddles us over to the riverbank, and once he's on solid ground he reaches down, clasps my hand, and helps me up. I'm surprised to see that we haven't really floated all that far; the boathouse is just a hundred yards or so away. Nate picks up the inner tubes and slides his arms through the middle of each of them, then anchors them over his shoulders.

I follow him down a narrow dirt path, and when we reach the dock I slip on my shoes and wrap my towel around my shoulders. Nate throws the tubes in the boathouse and hurries back down to the dock. I hand him a towel after he puts his shirt on, and I shiver when the wind picks up, chilling me to the bone.

"Here," Nate says, draping his towel over me. He takes my bag and slings it over his shoulder, then wraps his arm around me and tucks me into his side, blocking most of the wind and a good bit of the rain.

We walk back to the house at a fast clip. Nate, who's soaking wet, and me, feeling warmer than I can ever remember.

Chapter FIVE

I take a shower after we return from the river, all the while thinking over what Nate said to me earlier; about being able to touch people's lives with the work that I do, even though it doesn't always feel that important while I'm doing it. He has an interesting perspective on life, and he makes me think. It's a little unsettling that I find myself wanting to seek him out just to talk to him, to listen to the things that he has to say.

It's almost time for dinner, so I get dressed and head out into the hallway, ready to make my way to the main house. Of course I run into Ethan. I'm tempted to turn and retreat into my room, but I need to get this over with. I haven't really spoken to him since he's been here, apart from a quick hello on the day he arrived.

He's wearing a yellow button-down shirt and a pair of loose-fitting khakis. I've seen that shirt before; I bought it for him when we first moved in together. I doubt he remembers that I'm the one who gave it to him.

"Hey," he says, rubbing his chin between his index finger and thumb. He always does that when he's nervous, and I hate that I can still read him. "How are you?"

"I'm doing well," I tell him. I know I should be polite and ask after him, but I don't really feel like being polite. I don't want to make this easy for him, don't want to talk to him like we're just old friends who haven't seen each other in a while.

"You look good," he says.

I should thank him, but I don't.

"Listen, Callie." He rubs his chin again. "I want to say thank you for letting me come here to the wedding. It means a lot to me."

Even though Gabby and Ben did ask me before they invited Ethan, I don't like the way he makes it seem like I'm the one running the show.

"If the situation had been reversed," I say, even though it guts me to consider myself doing anything similar to what he did to me, "I hope you would've done the same thing. It would've killed me if something that happened between you and me kept me from Gabby's wedding."

"I would've deserved it, if you hadn't wanted me to come." Even though I know from experience that Ethan is quite a good liar, I make the choice to believe him this time.

"I've never been vindictive, Ethan."

"I know that. It's one of the things I-" He stops himself before he says it. It's one of the things he loved about me. Loved, past tense. Past tense, like the two of us. And this is the moment when our breakup feels final to me. It wasn't when he cried, begging me to give him another chance. It wasn't when I packed all my things into boxes and put them in a cold, empty storage room. Not when he stopped by my mother's house three days later to return a pair of my earrings that he had found on the dresser. Now. Here. In a hallway in Virginia at our best friends' wedding.

It's over. And I'm okay with that.

"Your new girlfriend is pretty." I'm not really sure what possesses me to say it, but it feels right to be nice to him for some reason, for my own sake.

"I just want you to know, I only brought her with me because I knew I wasn't welcome with the group. I didn't want to come here and be alone when I wasn't hanging with Ben."

For the first time since our breakup, I feel bad for him. I know that he wants me to extend an offer to him to hang out with all of us, but I can't do it. It's not fair to his new girlfriend, Emily, to have to hang out with his ex, and it's not fair to myself to offer up something that I'm not ready to give. Maybe in time I can be around him, but not now.

"I should go see if I can help Amy with dinner," I say, ready to make my exit. I can't stand here and make small talk with him any longer. "Are you coming?"

"Yeah, later." Ethan offers me a small nod as I walk past him. "You look really good."

There are a thousand nasty responses I could make, but instead I settle for a simple thank you.

I turn and make my way down the hall. I can't see Ethan's face, but I know he's watching me walk away.

Chapter Six

The Wright home at dinnertime is unlike anything I'm used to. Coming from a single-parent household, dinner usually consisted of me throwing something frozen in the microwave and eating by myself while I finished my homework. Here, everyone is gathered together, engaging in conversation.

There is some familial bickering going on in the dining room just off the kitchen; Ben and Nate's sister Jessa arrived earlier this afternoon from Philly. She and her father are arguing about how much she should pay for the granite countertops she wants for the kitchen renovation that she and her husband are working on. I like Jessa; she's boisterous like her mother, and she doesn't take crap from either one of her brothers. She's gorgeous too, and at twenty-seven, she's the oldest of the Wright children.

Here in the kitchen, Amy has given me the task of making garlic bread. Truthfully, I'd do anything she asked me to. I love being around her; she makes me feel like part of her family. The lasagna that she made is bubbling away in the oven, smelling so good that I have to stop myself from walking over there, opening the door, and shoveling handfuls into my mouth while it's still cooking. I bet the burns would be worth it, that's how good it smells.

"There's this park in New York that was built on old train tracks," Amy says enthusiastically as she fills a pot with water. "It's so gorgeous and green among the concrete buildings of the city. I think I'm going to take the train up this spring and have a nice, long visit. You should come." She looks over at Gabby.

I pick up a dollop of butter with my knife and spread it on the bread, trying not to feel so left out because the two of them are on the other side of the kitchen making plans without me. It's not like I'm a member of this family, so I have no rational reason to be jealous. Still, I am.

"We could make a weekend out of it," Amy says as she scrubs the pot.

Gabby is busy slicing carrots for the salad. "Yeah, that'd be fun."

"Callie?"

I look up, expecting Amy to correct my butter-spreading technique, but she's just staring at me expectantly.

"I'm sorry?" I have no idea what she's waiting for.

"Would you be up for a girls' weekend in New York? We could see a show or something."

I look over at Gabby, who is just smiling down at the salad bowl.

"I'd like that," I say, unable to stop my ridiculous grin.

"We'd have to go to a spa or something, do it up right," Amy says, and I can tell that the prospect of this trip is going to fuel her for the next few months. She is definitely the type to put together a whole itinerary on her own, and having someone else plan things for me makes the trip sound all that much more exciting. Amy is so organized that I want to take her aside and ask her if she'd mind taking a look at my life. See if she can put things in order.

Once I've finished with the garlic bread, I ask Amy if there's anything else I can do to help with dinner.

"Nope," she says, looking over at Gabby with a conspiratorial grin. "Why don't you go out into the living room and meet Madeline?"

Madeline is Jessa's daughter, and I just so happen to know that she's out in the living room playing with her Uncle Nate. The very last thing I need to see in this world is that beautiful man with a small child. Amy and Gabby must know that, and because they're both evil, evil women, they insist I go out there, grinning all the while.

"You two are about as subtle as an anvil to the head," I say as I head to the door.

I can hear them giggling behind me as I walk out of the kitchen.

*I*n the living room, Nate is sitting cross-legged in front of a child-sized table, which is covered by a pink tablecloth with tiny purple flowers embroidered all over it. A hot pink feather boa is wrapped around his neck. It's tiny, meant for someone Madeline's size.

"Pinky up, Uncle Nate!" Madeline says. She sounds exhausted, like she's told Nate to remember his manners a thousand times before. He complies immediately, gently lifting the tiny purple tea cup from the tiny purple saucer that he's holding in his right hand.

He sees me standing in the doorway and he smiles. He smiles without a hint of embarrassment, without even reaching to pull off the boa or set down the cup. It's like he's living for this little girl's amusement, and I have to admit that's so incredibly endearing.

"Mad," he says, nodding in my direction. "You have a customer."

Madeline grabs an old notepad from the pocket of the tiny checkered apron that's tied around her waist, and she rushes over to me.

"Welcome," she says, pulling a pencil from behind her ear. "How many?"

"Just one," I reply.

"This way."

Nate grins as his niece leads me toward him, and I sit cross-legged on the floor, mirroring him.

"Nice boa," I say.

"My purple one's at the cleaners," he replies, tossing it over his shoulder.

"Well, pink looks good on you."

Nate puts the cup and the saucer down on the table. "You know, I've heard that before." He offers me a sly grin.

"I'll bet you have."

Madeline walks up to the table, her oversized pencil at the ready. "Coffee or tea?"

"Tea please."

She clinks her tiny tea kettle against my tiny cup and pours it to the brim with air.

"Maddie," Nate says. "This is Miss Callie. Callie, this is my niece Madeline."

"Hi Miss Callie," Madeline replies, completely disinterested. Her laser-like focus on her fake cafe operation is so cute, and I can't help but smile at her even as she snubs me.

Nate isn't having any of that behavior though. "What do we say?" His voice is so patient, and still kind.

Madeline turns her body toward me, but looks over at Nate. Out of the corner of my eye I can see him mouthing words to her.

"Nice to meet you, Miss Callie." She's staring at Nate as she says the words, nodding her head after each one of them.

"It's nice to meet you," I tell her.

"Good girl," Nate says, beaming at Madeline. She walks over to him and wraps her arms around his neck as she leans in and whispers something in his ear, giggling.

Nate raises himself up to his knees before he stands. "I'll be back in a sec."

My eyes grow wide with low-level panic. "I don't know what to do with kids."

"Just talk to her. She's like a tiny adult. You just can't cuss in front of her."

Nate glances back at me as he walks out of the room. I watch Madeline play in the makeshift kitchen she and Nate built out of couch cushions and blankets. She's wearing a tiny broncos jersey, one that Nate has no doubt given to her. It's too long, almost like a dress on her.

"I like your jersey," I say, trying to start a conversation. "Do you watch a lot of football?"

She nods. "With Daddy."

"Do you play?" I ask, half teasing, just wanting to know how she'll respond.

She turns around and looks at me like I've just said the most ridiculous thing in the world. Pointing at the sparkly crown she's wearing, she laughs. "Silly. Princesses don't play football!"

"Sure they do. They just have to strap on their tiaras."

Madeline laughs as she reaches over and hands me a plate with a plastic hot dog and a plastic can of peas on top of it, and I notice Nate standing in the doorway, grinning.

"We're training her to be a quarterback," he says as he walks over and sits down next to me. "She's got quite an arm on her."

"I made you a sammich," Madeline says, handing Nate a plate full of random plastic food.

"Looks delicious." He rubs his stomach, and I love the way he plays along with her. The way he doesn't care how ridiculous he looks or what he has to go along with in order to make this little girl happy. He brings the "sandwich" to his mouth and makes loud, exaggerated eating noises, then hides the plate under the table.

"You ated it all!" Madeline shouts, laughing.

"I did, and it was delicious. I want to meet the chef!"

"*I'm* the chef." Madeline points at her chest and Nate takes her by the arm, gently pulling her to him. He smothers her with kisses and her peals of laughter bounce off the walls. It's the best sound. With Madeline still laughing uncontrollably, Nate stands up and spins her around, increasing the laughter tenfold.

"Nate, be careful," Amy shouts from the other room. "It's time for dinner, and I'm not cleaning up any barf tonight."

"That's really appetizing, Mom. Thanks," Nate says.

"You already ate!" Madeline tells him with a giggle.

"I have room for more."

"Where?" She pats Nate's stomach, feeling around for some extra space.

"I have a hollow leg," he tells her, and the look on her face is priceless. "All the food goes down there when I eat it, so I have more room in my belly."

"Wow," Madeline sighs with wonder, eyes wide.

"Ready for dinner?" he asks her, and she nods enthusiastically. "Why don't you help Miss Callie get up?"

Madeline holds out her hands to me, and I clasp them in mine. Then Nate wraps his hands around her waist and pulls her back. Her hands slip out of mine.

"Uncle Nate!" she screams, laughing.

"Try again," he replies, winking at me. She grabs my hand and he pulls her away again, then wraps her in his arms. "Where's all that upper-body strength, princess? We're going to have to start working on some bench presses." He lifts her up over his head, and I have never seen a child having so much fun in my entire life.

"Nate!" Amy warns.

Madeline holds out her hand again, and I clasp it in mine. I take Nate's hand with my free one, and he pulls me up. Madeline runs into the living room, and the smile that Nate wears as he watches her takes my breath away. And I could kill Amy and Gabby for subjecting me to all of this cuteness.

"C'mon," Nate says, his hand gently pressing into the small of my back as he leads me to the dining room.

Mr. and Mrs. Wright are sitting next to each other, with Jessa and Madeline directly across from them. Ethan and Emily are at the far end, thankfully. There are only two empty chairs left, and they're right next to each other, which I'm sure is no accident. Nate pushes my chair in as I sit down, and then he takes the seat to my left. When I look up, I notice Ethan watching the two of us, and I can't lie, I feel a twinge of satisfaction at the hint of jealousy I see in his eyes.

Gabby and Ben sit across from Nate and me, too wrapped up in each other to notice that there's an actual meal taking place. They look so in love that it'd be sickening if they weren't my friends.

Jessa is thinking the same thing I am. "You two look so in love," she says, sighing a little as she cuts into her lasagna. "I remember that look. It starts to fade a bit when you're running after a screaming four-year-old."

"Oh shush," Amy says, flipping her napkin at her daughter. "Your father and I had the three of you, and we still look at each other like that."

"Which is a miracle after having Nate," Jessa replies.

Nate gives her a playful sneer. "Clearly I wasn't too bad since Mom and Dad had another kid after me." He looks over at Ben dismissively. "They stopped after you, so…"

"Only because they had achieved perfection," Ben says, puffing out his chest. "Besides, if they could survive Jess's projectile vomiting, they can survive anything."

Jessa laughs. "You haven't seen projectile vomiting until-"

"Vomit!" Madeline shouts.

"That's enough," Mr. Wright—Jack—says, looking both disgusted and amused at the same time. "Every conversation this family has seems to devolve into one about bodily functions."

"And yet Nate, Jess and I are still here," Ben says, picking up his glass of wine. "There must've been some real magic in the air the night you and Mom met."

"How did you meet?" I ask.

There's a collective groan from the three Wright children.

"Now you've done it," Ben says.

Amy rolls her eyes. "You all seem to have a lot of opinions for people who wouldn't exist if it wasn't for that night."

"Well, I'd like to hear about it," I say.

"Thank you Callie," Amy replies, and I can tell from the smile on her face that she just loves telling people this story. The exasperated looks on the faces of her children prove that she tells it often.

"I was an exchange student in Paris." There's a far-off look in her eyes and a soft grin on her lips. "I was looking for this tiny art house theater. I fancied myself to be quite the movie snob back then. I had been searching for it for close to an hour, using a map that someone had drawn on a cocktail napkin. I asked around, but my French wasn't good enough to be able to understand the directions that people were giving me. I was so lost, and then I snagged my purse handle on the end of a bench. When I bent down to pick it up, I noticed that another set of hands was reaching for it. They belonged to Jack." She looks over at her husband and cups his face before threading her fingers through his. And even though I'm sure he's heard this story a thousand times, he still looks completely taken by her. "He knew where the theater was; he'd been there countless times before. We went to a small bistro down the street from the theater, and we ended up missing the movie. We talked until the bistro closed."

"Until they kicked us out," Jack says, smiling tenderly as he looks at his wife.

Amy grins at him and squeezes his hand. "He walked me home to my apartment."

"I walked by there every day on my way to class. I always knew something was special about that building." Jack touches his forehead to Amy's, and I swear it's one of the sweetest things I've ever seen.

"We've been together ever since. Managed to bring these three goofballs into the world," Amy says, laughing.

"You wouldn't know what to do without us," Jessa replies as she cuts up Madeline's lasagna.

Amy looks at me. "I always like to say that meeting Mr. Wright was-"

"The best thing that ever happened to me," Jessa, Nate and Ben reply in unison, sounding pretty unenthusiastic about the events that led up to their existence. They're obviously teasing their mother, and she rolls her eyes at them. Jack leans over and gives her a soft kiss, and it's touching to see something so simple and romantic between two people who have been together for so many years.

"I hope you feel the same way, Gabby," Amy says.

"I do," Gabby replies, taking Ben's hand.

"This is so beautiful." Emily dabs at her eyes, and everyone at the table turns and looks at her, completely surprised that she said something.

Nate, unfortunately, is the first person to reply. "It really is beautiful," he says, looking pointedly at Ethan. "Stories about men who honor their commitments are few and far between these days."

I pinch Nate's leg under the table, while Ethan looks like he'd love nothing more than for the floor to open up and swallow him whole.

*A*fter dinner, Nate and I stand side-by-side at the sink. He's washing the dirty pots and pans, and I'm arranging the dinner plates into neat rows in the dishwasher. I've been stewing over the comment he made to Emily about commitment since he said it, trying to figure out whether or not I should say something to him about it. But Nate has his shirt sleeves rolled up, and I keep getting distracted by his forearms, watching them dip in and out of the suds, all soaking wet and strong and beautiful.

I really should splash myself with some of that dishwater to get my mind right before I open my mouth, but the two of us are alone and with a house full of people and a wedding on the way, who knows when that will happen again? I need to take my chance while I have it.

"Listen," I say as I rearrange a few coffee cups to make room for another one to fit on the rack. "I don't need you to stick up for me."

"What do you mean?" Nate asks, turning off the water and drying his hands with a dishtowel.

"I mean that I don't want this week to be uncomfortable. I don't want to have to worry about someone bringing up the past and throwing it in Ethan's face or throwing it in mine."

Nate turns to me, and for some strange reason I want to reach up and smooth over the crease between his furrowed brows. "I wasn't trying to throw the past in anyone's face, Callie."

I sigh, not really sure if I'm explaining things so that he'll understand where I'm coming from. "Maybe that wasn't the best way to put it. It's just that what happened between Ethan and me, it happened between *Ethan* and *me*. And now I'm in this awkward position of being here and trying to keep my distance while he's still a part of things because his friends are my friends. It's difficult, and I don't want to worry about it more than I have to. I don't want to worry about you saying something that's going to bring all of that out into the open. Maybe it's just better to let it be."

Nate's arm grazes mine, and it sends a shiver through my body that makes my stomach flip. "I know we only just met and I don't know all that much about you, but…" When our eyes meet, he takes a deep breath and purses his lips, seemingly reconsidering whatever it is that he was going to say. That, of course, makes me entirely too curious.

"But what?"

Nate's eyes search mine, and it's so easy for me to get lost in that deep, expressive blue. He shakes his head, and the corner of his mouth quirks up in a half-smile.

"Nothing," he replies, and turns his focus back on the dishes.

Chapter
SEVEN

After Nate and I finish cleaning up the dinner mess, he goes upstairs and reads Madeline a bedtime story. Once she's all tucked in and sound asleep, Nate, Ben, Gabby and I all head over to the patio that's connected to the guest house. It's a beautiful outdoor space with a roof and open sides. There's a grilling area that's nicer than most of the kitchens I've been in, and a large stone fireplace on the side of the patio that's opposite the house. Two love seats are positioned in front of the hearth; Ben and Gabby are all cuddled up in one, while Nate and I sit in the other, maybe an inch or so between us.

I'm settled into the cushions and my eyes are closed. I love the tickle of the wind blowing strands of hair across my face, and I take long, deep breaths. I can't remember the last time I've ever breathed like this. Like it's something I want to do rather than need to do.

"You really love this place, don't you?" Ben asks.

Gabby asked me the same thing yesterday, and I realize that I should probably be a little less obvious about it, lest one of the Wrights get worried that I'm going to want to stay forever. But tonight is not the night that I'm going to do that.

"Yes," I breathe, tilting my head toward the breeze before I open my eyes. "How did you guys ever leave it?"

"It's easy to leave a place when you know you can come back to it whenever you want," Nate replies with a grin. The small size of the love seat doesn't leave either of us much room, but I welcome the warmth from the close proximity of his body as I fold my legs underneath me, trying to keep out the chill.

"What Nate said." Ben wraps his arms around Gabby and she snuggles against his chest. I feel the familiar prick of jealousy beneath my skin. Not because I want Ben, but because I miss the feeling of being wrapped up in someone like that, completely trusting them with my heart, my life…my everything.

"Colorado, though," Nate says, looking over at me. "This place has nothing on Colorado."

"What made you choose to live there?" I ask.

There's a far-off look in his eyes, like he misses the place already. It's a look that makes my heart twist. He's too beautiful for that kind of longing, and I have to press my hands into fists to keep from reaching out for him. What is it about him that just draws me like a magnet?

"I went to CU on a scholarship for lacrosse, and the moment I stepped off the plane I just knew I was supposed to be there. It felt like home. I loved all the mountains, the lakes. Everything," Nate says.

Ben interjects with a little bit of brotherly teasing. "Nate's always liked to climb things just to jump off of them. Colorado's got plenty of things to jump off of."

"That's crazy," I say, laughing. I can't even wrap my mind around the kind of hobbies Nate must have. Rappelling, mountain climbing. Personally, I like having my feet firmly planted on the ground at all times. I don't really like taunting gravity by throwing myself off tall things.

"No." Nate looks over at me, his eyebrows scrunched together. The reflection from the firelight dancing on his face makes his expression very warm. "What's crazy is knowing there's so much beauty in this world and not actively seeking it out."

"You don't have to climb a mountain in order to appreciate how beautiful it is," I tell him.

"That's true, but the view is so much better from the top." Nate leans forward, resting his elbows on his knees. "I like to hike in this place called Willow Lakes. Get up really early and walk the trails when the air is still crisp, and the water is so still the reflections are like you're looking at the mountains through a mirror. It'll change your life."

He says that like he wants to take me there. Like one day he thinks he will.

"Callie can use a life change," Gabby says. "Maybe you could show her sometime."

"I could show you lots of things," Nate replies, his voice very soft and low. He's looking at me like I'm the only person in the world.

Unable to break his gaze, my breath catches in my throat and I have to work very hard to swallow it down.

"Callie doesn't do so well in nature." Typical Ben, breaking the tension. This time I'm grateful for it.

"I do fine in nature," I argue. "As long as nature leaves me alone." I can tell this is the beginning of Story Time with Gabby and Ben, featuring the tales of Callie vs. Mother Nature. There are so many stories to choose from.

Gabby looks over at me and rolls her eyes. "Nate, you're lucky you even got her out on the river the other day."

"Luck had nothing to do with it." He's talking to Gabby, but he's looking at me. The corners of his mouth tilt up into a sly grin that makes my stomach flutter.

I want to reach over and clasp my hand over Gabby's mouth to get her to shut up. I want to tell her that it wasn't luck that got me out on that river, it was her stupid scheming. I can't believe she's being so obvious in her quest to set up Nate and me. Not that it really matters that much considering both of us are on to her. But I don't want him to be uncomfortable, and, more importantly, I don't want to be uncomfortable either.

"I can be pretty charming," Nate says, being pretty charming. He leans back into the couch cushions before he stretches his legs out in front of him.

I reach down and pick up one of my flip flops and playfully toss it at him. He laughs, the jerk. The beautiful, charming jerk.

"I'm keeping this," he says, holding up my flip flop like it's some kind of prized possession.

"Good." I playfully stick my tongue out at him.

"Where does this deep-seated fear of adventure come from?" Nate sets my flip flop on his leg and runs the pad of his thumb along the flowered pattern on the strap.

"Don't ask her," Gabby teases. "She's got a list of aversions about a mile long."

"That's not true!"

She side eyes me, and all my rage melts away into laughter.

"Well, it's mostly not true." I guess I can't really deny that they've got me on this one.

"It's pretty true," Ben says.

"Not you too," I reply, glaring at him. "Is this gonna be what it's like when you're married? The two of you ganging up on me?"

"Let me tell him the story about spring break sophomore year." Ben is practically begging, and the desperation in his voice is so irritating. "About the lake."

I shrug, kind of defeated, and Ben takes this as a yes.

He looks over at Nate before he starts the story that is surely going to embarrass the hell out of me. "We went to some lake in central Texas during spring break." Nate seems entirely too interested in this story for my comfort. "We'd been drinking a little, and Ethan-" Ben stops in his tracks, as if mentioning Ethan's name is going to make him appear out of thin air.

"Keep going," I tell him, trying not to sound as irritated as I feel. He's already brought it up, there's no point in stopping now.

Ben, to his credit, hesitates before picking up where he left off, wanting to make sure that I'm okay with it before he continues. At this point I feel kind of trapped. If I tell him to stop I seem like a bad sport, if I let him keep going, well…I guess I'm about to find out what happens with that.

"Ethan had been badgering her to get on this tire swing the whole weekend. It was kind of like the one grandpop had at that lake near his house, remember?"

Nate nods and looks over at me for a fleeting moment before turning his attention back to his brother.

"Anyway," Ben continues, "it was hanging off of this tree-"

"It was a freaking huge tree on the edge of a cliff," I say, interrupting. I want to clarify the situation so this story sounds a little less ridiculous than I'm sure it's going to sound with Ben telling it.

"It wasn't a cliff, Callie," Ben laughs.

"It was a cliff," I tell Nate, even though I know that he thinks I'm exaggerating. I'm not. Well, I *am*, but only a little.

"Callie finally got the nerve to get on it, and Ethan pushed her off."

"He *shoved* me off," I say, glaring at Ben. He was there, he knows that's not an exaggeration. I had forgotten about what a jerk Ethan could be sometimes, even before the cheating.

"And she went flying, screaming her head off. We were all yelling at her to let go, but she waited too long and the tire had slowed down to the point where she just kind of slid out of it." Ben is killing himself laughing, and Gabby isn't all that far behind him. I know I looked ridiculous back then, but I can't help but feel like the two of them are such assholes for laughing at me, both then and now. My cheeks grow hot, and I tell myself that I'm just embarrassed at the story in general, not necessarily because it's being told in front of Nate.

I chance a glance over at him, worried that he's laughing too. But he's not. He looks like he wants to kick Ben's ass actually.

"So, she was just hanging there from the bottom of this tire swing, screaming," Ben continues.

"And you two assholes were laughing, just like you are now," I say, trying not to sound annoyed. I figure it's better for me to finish this story for the sake of my own sanity. "I finally let go and dropped down into this disgusting water that was full of eels. They all circled around me like they were guarding the entrance to hell." I shiver, wanting to throw up at the memory of the slimy feeling of them slithering across my legs. So disgusting.

"The entrance to hell?" Nate says, finally cracking a smile.

"Yes," I reply, nodding. "If there's a hell, the gates to it are guarded by eels, I'm sure of it." I rub my arms with my hands, trying to warm myself. I should be warm enough with all the anger and embarrassment coursing through my veins, but I'm not.

Nate sits forward and unbuttons the long-sleeved shirt he's wearing over a tee, then he slips the shirt over my shoulders.

"Won't you be cold?" I ask.

He grins and shakes my head. "Nah."

"Thank you," I reply. The shirt smells like him; that clean, comforting scent that I remember from our night together in Dallas. It takes everything I have in me not to bury my face in the collar and breathe deeply. "I guess the moral of the story is that A, I need some new friends. And B, I'm never getting into water where I can't see my feet ever again."

Nate's fingers brush along the cuff of his shirt that I'm wearing. "You did yesterday." My eyes meet his and he gives me a soft smile.

"Yeah, I guess I did." I'm surprised I didn't realize that before now.

He leans in so close to me that I can feel his warm breath on my cheek. "When you're around me, I think you'll wind up doing a lot of things that you thought you never would."

I'm not quite sure why, but I have a feeling that he's right.

Chapter
EIGHT

"I'm not sure how I feel about this," I say as a very patient hairdresser named Josephine smooths a few strands of Gabby's hair back into the most simple, elegant updo that I've ever seen. "I think maybe you need a great big flower right here." I point at the side of Gabby's head and she swats my hand away, smiling.

"Be serious, Callie. What do you think?" Gabby asks, looking up at me hopefully.

"I think that if I had every hairstyle in the world to choose for you to wear on your wedding day, I'd choose this one." I gently put my hand on her shoulder, and she reaches up and gives it a squeeze.

"This is perfect, Josephine," Gabby says, turning her head to admire herself in the mirror.

"It'll look so elegant with the bodice of your dress." Amy is standing behind Gabby, smiling at her reflection.

Gabby attempts a smile in return, but it's a sad one that doesn't quite stick. I recognize that look in her eyes; I've seen it a hundred times over the course of the past few years. As a mother, Amy must recognize it too, because she takes Josephine aside to finalize arrangements for the wedding prep on Saturday morning. I'm careful not to comfort Gabby while someone else is in the room, because I know how she feels about people making a fuss over her. But I want so badly to hug her, to show her so much love that she can't possibly feel any of the pain. I want to guard her against unpleasant thoughts and build a wall around her so tall that no bittersweet memories can find their way in. Only happiness and love.

As if Gabby can sense that I want to hug her, she shakes her head and grabs a tissue off of the vanity as she stands up. She's very careful to avoid looking me in the eye, and I wonder if it's because she thinks she'll cry if she does. Whatever makes things easier for her, that's what I want to do.

"Updo for the bride and curls for the bridesmaids," Josephine says, confirming our hairstyles with Amy as she reads off of the notepad she's holding. "I'll be here at eight sharp."

Amy looks back at me and Gabby, understanding that we need a few minutes alone together. "I'll walk you out," she says, following Josephine through the door of the guest room that she's designated for bridal party wedding preparations.

Then it's just the two of us in the room, which is all decked out with mirrors and makeup tables for the big day. And while I'm looking around and noticing all the special touches Amy has put in place to make sure that everything's perfect for the wedding, I feel this sudden rush of affection for her. She's a caring woman anyway, and I know she loves Gabby, but she's going out of her way to make sure that Gabby knows it. She needs to feel like she belongs to a family on this day more than others. Gabby walks behind a partition that's set up in the corner of the room, and I can hear the rustling of the dress bag her wedding gown is hanging in as she opens it. I'm not really sure what to do or say that will make her feel better, so I sit down on the edge of the bed.

"Do you need any help?" I ask, desperate to break up the silence between us.

"Not yet." Her voice is a little shaky, and I can tell that she's so desperately trying to keep it together.

Knowing her as well as I do, I want to tell her that it's okay to cry. But deep down inside I know that won't help anything. Instead I try to shift her focus to what she's gaining in order to take it away from what she's missing.

"You're marrying into a really great family, Gab," I say quietly. "They all love you so much."

She doesn't answer, but she doesn't really have to. I know that she is well aware of how everyone in the Wright family feels about her. Just as I'm about to run my mouth to start some kind of conversation, Gabby walks out from behind the partition with her head down, coming to a stop when she reaches the full-length mirror that's propped against the wall.

"Will you zip me up?"

I walk over to her and slowly pull up the zipper. This dress is so Gabby: elegant and understated. Gorgeous. Classic. It's a lovely lace and silk sheath dress with a sweetheart neckline, and the silhouette is absolutely perfect for her figure.

When the dress is zipped, I step in front of the mirror to get a good look at Gabby. The sun is shining through the window behind her and it bounces off of the mirror, casting a lovely glow over her face, and having her hair pulled back accentuates her high cheekbones and delicate features.

"Look at you," I say quietly, smiling through the tears that are welling up in my eyes. It seems like only yesterday that the two of us played dress-up in my mom's bedroom and pretended to be getting ready for our own weddings. And here she is, looking more beautiful than either one of us probably could've ever imagined. "You're so gorgeous, Gab."

It's those words that finally make her cry, probably because she wishes more than anything that her mother and father were here to say them.

"I miss them, Callie," she says, tears streaming down her cheeks. "I wish they were here." It's just so like her to try to hold it together, because she's always been the kind of person who felt like she had to be strong for everyone else, and that need intensified after they died. It happened exactly one month after Gabby's eighteenth birthday. Mr. and Mrs. Morgan left the house all dressed up for a night at the theater, but there was a thunderstorm and the roads were slick, and Mr. Morgan swerved just a second too late…

I was spending the night at her house, and was standing next to her when she opened the front door to two police officers who were offering their condolences. I rarely left her side during the rough months that followed. That kind of experience forms a bond between two people that's so thick that I don't even need her to tell me what she's going to say next. I already know, and I wish I could do something to make it come true for her.

"I'd give anything for them to be here," she whispers.

"I know you would," I say, wrapping my arms around her and holding her tight. I struggle to find the right words to say, not wanting to offer her some trite sentiment by telling her that they're in a better place somewhere watching over her. That kind of thinking is rarely a comfort to a person who would rather have her loved ones right here with her. "I love you," are the words that finally leave my mouth.

She's quiet a moment before she says, "I love you too." It takes her a while to let go of me, and when she pulls away she's smiling through her tears. She fans her face and quickly swipes her cheeks with the backs of her hands, and I have to smile at her. She never could handle too much emotion at once.

"Please unzip me so I can get out of this thing before I get mascara all over it."

I laugh as I imagine the shitstorm that would follow her realizing that she had a black smudge on her pristine white dress. After I unzip her, she walks back behind the screen in the corner of the room.

"Talk to me about something that won't make me cry," she says, sounding a little more like herself than she did before.

"Okay," I reply, wracking my brain to come up with another subject. I wind up saying the goofiest thing that comes to mind. "Would you still marry Ben if he sounded like a chipmunk?"

I think her laugh is the most beautiful sound I've ever heard.

Chapter
NINE

*I*t's close to midnight when I'm driven out of my bedroom by the unrelenting thumping of a headboard against my wall. Ethan has never really been all that wild in bed, so either he's trying to antagonize me in the tackiest way ever, or his new girlfriend is seriously rocking his world. I know that he wants me to *think* she is, at least. With him, anything is possible. Regardless of the reason for the late-night interruption, I don't want to listen to it.

Since I'm not going to be able to get any sleep at this point, I might as well try to get some work done. My windows are open and the breeze floating through them is a pleasant kind of cool, so I grab my laptop and make my way outside, hoping that I'll be able to get a wifi signal out there. I walk out onto the patio and over to the fireplace, flipping the switch that I saw Nate use to turn it on last night. The hammock hanging between the pillars on the right side of the porch practically calls to me, so I plop myself down onto it and flip open my computer.

I squint against the brightness of the screen out here in the dark, but it doesn't take long for my eyes to adjust. Luckily I'm able to sign onto the family's network. There are a few web development quotes in my inbox, so I take a look at my calendar to figure out if I can fit the work into my schedule. After I respond to those clients, I pull up a project that's nearly finished. I play around with some font sizes and tweak a few colors until I'm almost satisfied with the end result.

"You gonna sleep out here?"

I'm so startled that I nearly fall out of the hammock, and manage to keep my laptop from crashing to the ground thanks to some surprisingly quick reflexes on my part. I was so lost in my work that I didn't even hear Nate approaching.

"I'm certainly not going to now," I say breathlessly, dramatically clutching my chest.

"I didn't mean to scare you," he says with a light chuckle as he walks around the far side of the hammock. "I saw that the fireplace was on and wanted to make sure that everything was on the up and up out here."

"In case I was a thief?" I ask, grinning.

"Thieves don't usually sit down and make themselves comfortable, but I guess you never know."

"Obviously a thief has never sat in this hammock."

Nate smiles as he slides his fingertips along the ropes. "Mind if I join you? This is usually my spot when I come home, but now it's been usurped by some…by some-"

"Stranger."

"No," he replies tenderly, shaking his head. "Definitely not that."

My heart skips a beat as he looks down at me with an undercurrent of longing. Before I can second guess myself, I move over to make room for him. As he eases onto the opposite side of the hammock, he accidentally brushes my foot with his arm.

"Jesus, Callie. Your feet are freezing."

"That's why I turned on the fireplace," I say, hurrying to finish the email I was working on when he interrupted me.

Nate hops off the hammock, walks over to a cabinet that's on the other side of the porch, and he pulls out a plush-looking blanket. He unfolds it as he walks toward me and he spreads it over me before he lowers himself back into the hammock. I can't help but smile at how attentive he is; he always seems to be so completely aware of what it is I need, which is remarkable considering I've only known him for a few days. I decide not to dwell on that fact, because thinking about how sweet he is will get me in trouble.

"Thank you," I say, loving the warmth against my bare legs and relishing in Nate's body heat as he slips beneath the blanket. He grins at me as he reaches over and pulls my feet onto his chest. He rubs them, working out the dull ache there like it isn't even a thing. A small sigh escapes my lips as I ignore my work and let my head rest against the ropes and enjoy the feeling of someone taking care of me. It's been forever since I felt anything like it.

"So," Nate says, grinning at me. "What are you doing down here?"

I take a deep breath and tap my chin with my index finger while I decide whether or not I want to tell him the truth.

"Let's just say that there was some noise in the room next to mine. I was worried that if I stayed in there any longer that I'd get sucked into some strange bad porn vortex."

Nate draws a breath through his nose, and as he continues rubbing my feet, his strokes have a little more pressure to them.

"Can I just say, without any personal agenda, that I'm really glad you broke up with that asshole?"

I nod and look down at my keyboard. I'm not really sure what to say to that.

"It's fucking tacky to do that to anyone, let alone someone you..." Nate trails off, shaking his head. "Sorry, things like that just piss me off."

"If it makes you feel any better, there was an over-the-top enthusiasm to the banging that made me think it wasn't authentic. And the moaning was... theatrical."

Nate laughs. "The pounding shows a lack of finesse. And I think it takes more talent to make a woman feel so good that she can't make any noise at all."

My cheeks flush as I look up at him, and his eyes are so intense when they look into mine. My breath catches as I remember that night I spent with him, the times when he made me feel so good that I couldn't breathe, couldn't move, couldn't make a sound. Having accomplished his mission of getting me all flustered, Nate changes the subject.

"What are you working on?" he asks, like he didn't just set my world spinning.

I take a deep breath to steady my pounding heart. "Just a few quotes for some site work. I don't usually take time off, and I'm really scared of falling behind. Just a day or two more of turnaround time can make the difference between a really happy customer and a really angry one."

Nate nods, resting the back of his head against the hammock. "I thought one of the great things about being your own boss was getting to take time off whenever you wanted to."

"Not when you have a small business," I reply, laughing. Time off? Is he kidding? "Although it is kind of cool to be able to work from wherever I want."

"Except your bedroom up there," he says with a crooked smile.

"Except my bedroom."

"Can I see what you're working on?" He nods in the direction of my laptop.

"No," I reply softly with a grin. I close my laptop's lid. It wouldn't be a big deal to let him see a few of my projects, but I'm way too self-conscious about my work and I'm worried about what I would do if he didn't like my designs. Ridiculous as it may be, I feel like it would crush me a little.

If my reaction bothers him, he doesn't let on. "Do you have any advice for someone just starting a business?"

I raise my eyebrows because I'm kind of surprised at his question. "Why, are you thinking about starting one?"

"The friend I met in DC before I came here, he wants me to partner up with him to design a line of outdoor gear." Nate's fingers lay still on my feet, and I miss the kneading immediately. I also notice the way his eyes are downcast when he talks about this venture, which is a good indicator that he isn't too excited about it for whatever reason. And I want to know what that reason is.

"My first bit of advice is that you should probably be excited about your product if you have any hope at all of being successful selling it," I tease, gently nudging him with my knee.

It takes a long while for his eyes to meet mine. "I am," he says when he finally looks at me. "It's just that my dad thinks it's a waste of time. He's not really being very supportive."

"If he's anything like my mom, he just worries about you. Back when they were younger, starting a business wasn't as big of a gamble as it is now. It was a gamble, don't get me wrong, but not like today. They don't understand that we don't have the options that they did. The corporate environment is so different now, and with every company cutting costs and maxing out their workforce, it's not enough just to work hard and be the best. It's difficult to move up. To move anywhere," I tell him. "Sometimes you need to take things into your own hands. Or try to, at least."

Immediately his expression softens, and instinctively I know that I've said the right thing. Nate gets back to work on my feet, and I take a deep breath and sigh as he hits a sore spot that needed some attention.

"I like my job," he explains. "I just want to try something new."

"I think you should do it. Do you have a name picked out?"

"Kyle—my friend—he likes Rocky Mountain Rec, but...I don't know."

"I like it too." It doesn't even take me ten seconds to start mentally configuring logo ideas, even though Nate hasn't given me the slightest indication that he's at all interested in my input. "It's simple, it rolls off the tongue. Conveys the purpose of the company," I say, finishing the sentence with a yawn.

Nate gives me a soft grin before he gently pats my foot. "C'mon," he says, swinging his legs over the side of the hammock. Once he's standing, he offers me his hand. I'm too tired to argue and too intrigued not to take it.

"Where are we going?" I let him pull me up. He takes my laptop, then walks over and shuts off the fireplace.

"Back to the house, to a porn-free room where it's nice and quiet. You can sleep in my room tonight. I'll take the floor. And tomorrow morning I'll ask Mom to give you a new room."

"You don't have to do that," I say, blinking my sandy, tired eyes.

"I know." He smiles at me, and it's such a beautiful sight that I just stand up and follow him into the main house.

I follow Nate through the kitchen, and the house is eerily quiet compared to how loud it usually is in here when the Wright clan is together. I do my best not to make any noise, so I tiptoe quietly across the floor because I'm worried about waking someone.

"I'm the only one who has a room down here," Nate explains. He's not exactly talking in his normal voice, and the softness in the inflection makes me smile. "No one can hear us."

He leads me into the living room, with its movie-screen-sized television and wood beamed ceiling, then down a long hallway. Snapshots in vintage frames decorate the walls, and part of me wants to ask him to slow down so I can get a good look at them. But my eyes are heavy, and there's time to look tomorrow.

"This is me," Nate says, leading me through a door at the end of the hallway that's slightly open. He reaches over and flips on the lights, and I grin when I see the inside of his room. I know he grew up here, and I was expecting bunk beds and posters of half-naked women; you know, typical teen boy stuff. But this room doesn't look like it ever belonged to a teenager. Either Amy redid it after Nate went off to college, or he's always had good taste.

The walls are a deep beige color, and dark wooden bookcases line the wall opposite the door. The bookcases hold stacks and stacks of books. Some are on their sides, some are lined up by size, tallest to shortest. The spines are all well-worn, and I like the fact that he's a reader. It's not something I've thought to ask, but it's nice to know. Instead of the half-naked model posters I was expecting to see, there are pictures of lakes and mountains. Posters of snowboarders and skiers. Sporting equipment is leaning against and perched on nearly every piece of furniture. Skis, a hockey stick, a tennis racket. Even if I didn't know that Nate manages a sporting goods store, I would be able to guess it based on the sheer amount of stuff that he has.

Nate's bed is huge, and it's perfectly made. I can't help but wonder if that's his handiwork or if Amy comes in here every morning when he's home and makes his bed for him. I can see either scenario being true.

"The bathroom's in here," Nate says, pushing open the door beside him. "I'll try to remember to put the seat down for you." He winks so that I know he's kidding, and when I lean against the doorway to take a peek inside, I can't believe how huge the bathroom is. Beautiful tile work with an open shower, like something you'd see in a design magazine. This is definitely something Amy and Jack had done recently. No way did this place look like it does now when Nate was in high school.

He walks over to his closet and pulls out a comforter and two pillows, then he spreads the comforter out on the floor. He steps around the makeshift bed and pulls down the sheets on his actual bed, making room for me. He fluffs the pillows with a dramatic thwack, and then he holds out his arms.

"It's all yours," he says.

I climb onto the bed, and it's softer than I thought it would be. My knees sink into the featherbed as I crawl over to the other side, and I find that I'm glad that Ethan had tacky loud sex with his new girlfriend, because this mattress is much nicer than the one in my guest room. I try to tell myself that my comfort here has nothing to do with the fact that Nate's so close. He pulls the covers up over me, and then his eyes meet mine, a tender smile on his face. His gaze lingers, and I get the feeling that there's something he wants to say, but instead he just whispers "Goodnight."

"Goodnight."

Nate's fingertips slide along the duvet, and then he turns and walks into the bathroom, shutting the door behind him. I turn onto my side and watch the shadows of his feet in the slit beneath the door. The whole bed smells like him, and I turn my head against the pillow and breathe in. It's not cologne or anything you can buy, it's some combination of clean and outdoorsy that's uniquely him, and I want to bottle it so I can bring it home with me. Somehow I get the feeling that smell wouldn't be nearly as attractive if Nate wasn't around, but I push that thought down deep.

Nate walks out of the bathroom wearing a grey tee and navy blue shorts, and when he reaches over to turn out the light, I call his name.

"Yeah?"

"You don't have to sleep down there," I say, pursing my lips together as I pull the sheet back to make room for him to get in.

"Are you sure?"

I'm sure that this is probably a stupid move on my part. But I want him in this bed next to me, I can't deny that.

"You've already been inside of me," I say, trying to tease him. "Sharing a bed is nothing."

When his eyes meet mine, my intended joke seems a little too serious. But Nate's mouth quirks up in a half smile, and he climbs in anyway.

I'm on my side and he's on his back, though I can tell he wants to turn toward me. Maybe because I'm in the bed or maybe because he always sleeps that way, I don't know. He looks over at me and I grin, hoping he'll understand that it's okay for him to move. We're being all awkward about this like a couple of teenagers; it's kind of cute and definitely maddening. Finally he turns toward me, his eyes still locked with mine, and I can't look away. I don't want to. The moonlight shining through the window behind me casts the most beautiful light on his face. Bluish and kind of dreamy, like I'm in some kind of a haze. Nate smiles this comfortable, lazy smile, like there's nowhere in the world he'd rather be than here in this bed with me.

"Are you going to be here when I wake up?" he asks.

It could've been a vindictive question, given the way I behaved the last time we were like this. But he asks it so softly that it sounds more like a wish than anything.

"Yes," I whisper.

He watches me for a moment, then he reaches over and tucks a strand of hair behind my ear, his fingertips gently sliding down my cheek. His touch leaves a hot trail on my skin, leaves me wanting more. It's a dangerous, wonderful feeling. He pulls his hand away quickly, a glint of regret flashing across his face. I don't like that look; I much prefer the smile I saw only moments earlier.

Maybe it's because I miss just sleeping with someone, or maybe it's because I miss the feeling of someone else's skin, I don't know. But I reach over and twine my fingers with Nate's, clasping our hands together.

I close my eyes and sleep more soundly than I have in months.

Chapter
TEN

The morning air is cool and breezy, and the sun is so bright in the sky, the promise of a beautiful day to come. Jessa, Ben, Gabby and Madeline are walking in front of us, cutting a new path across the soft green grass in the field behind the Wrights' house. Nate and I trail behind them, looking at each other every few steps and smiling. Sometimes he looks away first, and sometimes I do. But our eyes always end up on each other, and it makes this tingling warmth well up inside of me.

I had stayed with him last night, and I was still there in the morning, just like I promised I would be. We woke up all tangled together; his left arm was completely numb from me resting my head on it all night, and my foot was falling asleep from where it had gotten caught between his calves sometime in the middle of the night. He rubbed my foot as it regained feeling, and I slid my fingers down his arm, helping to wake it back up. We laughed and teased each other until we finally rolled out of bed, and when I left his room, I felt an ache not completely unlike the one I'd felt when I left him in the hotel early that morning after we'd slept together.

In the shower I had thought too long and too hard about what I should and shouldn't be feeling, and I promised myself I'd keep a distance from him, if for no other reason to protect my own heart. Then I saw him at breakfast, telling Madeline a silly story about trolls to get her to eat her eggs, and I knew I couldn't stay away. What difference does it make anyway? In four days he'll be going back to Colorado and I'll be going back to Texas, and that will be that. Is there anything wrong with enjoying this feeling while I can? I just have to be careful. I can be careful.

Jessa and Gabby are each holding one of Madeline's hands, swinging her through the air as they walk. I remember doing the same thing when I was young, back when my parents were still together. It's one of my earliest memories, and one of the only ones I have of us all together as a family. Madeline's high-pitched peals of laughter as she swings back and forth make it sound like she's having the time of her life.

"You know," Jessa says, "I remember a time when Mom and Dad were doing this with Benny, and his hands slipped out of theirs. He landed flat on his back." She laughs in a way that any sister would at the misfortune of one of her younger siblings.

"So that's what happened," Nate says, looking at his sister like that's a legitimate explanation for something he's always thought was wrong with Ben.

"Well, if you ask me, I think Nate definitely shows classic signs of being dropped on his head," Ben says.

"No one asked you," Nate replies, laughing. He winks at me before he looks ahead, and my insides flutter.

Ben ignores him. "Remember when he shaved it back in middle school? So lumpy." He looks back at his brother, pointing to his head.

Nate feigns offense. "My head is near perfect in its head-like shape. And I looked awesome bald." He leans down so close to me that I can feel his stubble against the shell of my ear. "I really did."

With hair, without hair. I can't imagine Nate *not* looking good.

"Everyone looks awesome bald when it's by choice," Jessa says. "Once the Wright family male-pattern baldness shows up, you'll be singing a different tune."

"There's always Rogaine." Ben self-consciously rubs the back of his head.

Gabby tries to be discreet when she leans back to get a better look at his hair situation, and I have to laugh. Madeline breaks away from Gabby and Jessa and runs ahead of us, her long, curly brown hair flowing behind her. Jessa runs after her and tickles her when she finally catches up, and the two of them collapse onto the ground in a fit of laughter.

"I wanted to tell you," Gabby says, "Ben and I are going out to dinner with Ethan and Emily tonight." She slowly turns and looks at me, eyes wary, like she's nervous about my reaction. It's not like I expected her to spend all of her time with me. What was the point of inviting Ethan if he was just going to be relegated to unwelcome status, isolated from his best friend? I said I was okay with him coming, and I think I've acted like it so far.

"I hope you have fun," I tell her.

"Where in the hell are you going to dinner? The gas station off the main road?" Nate laughs at his joke, getting a kick out of himself. I can't lie, it's kind of adorable.

"Is there nothing around here?" I realize that I haven't stepped foot off of this property in the few days that I've been here, and I didn't really pay all that much attention on the ride to the house on the day I arrived.

"There's less than nothing around here," Nate explains. "Why do you think we have so much to do here at the house? It's a self-contained entertainment environment."

"We're going to a place just outside of Richmond," Ben says, like it's nothing to drive an hour away just to have dinner with his friend. Over the course of the past six months since Ethan and I broke up, I've wanted to hug Ben for being so great about the whole thing. For being on my side, but for managing to keep Ethan as a friend without ever condoning what he did.

"Hey," Nate says, sliding his hand down my arm to get my attention. His fingers leave a heated trail in their wake, and I shiver. "How would you feel about me making you dinner?"

Four days, Callie. Four days. Be *careful.*

I smile at him. "I'd feel pretty great about it."

*N*ate stands at the kitchen island, carefully cutting slices from a fresh loaf of bread. I have to admit that I'm really impressed with how seriously he's taking his offer to cook me dinner. I was expecting macaroni and cheese or some other bachelor speciality, but he's really trying here. Once he's finally satisfied with the bread, he places four slices on the cutting board, inspecting how fit they are for toasting. There's a plate full of cooked bacon resting on the stove, and my stomach is growling. I asked him if I could help earlier, in part to be polite and in part to speed this process along so we could eat. He flatly refused, preferring, in his words, that I "watch the master work."

"What are you-"

Nate turns and gently places his finger on my lips, then quietly shushes me.

"I need to concentrate, Callie," he says. I nearly laugh; it's so cute the way he's trying to turn sandwich making into an art.

He places the bread in the toaster, then starts slicing the tomato as precisely as he sliced the bread. He gets into a groove right about the time that Amy walks by the kitchen and then backtracks, stopping in the doorway.

"Sandwiches, Nate?" she asks, shaking her head. "That's not how you woo a lady."

Nate's shoulders slump and he drops the knife on the cutting board. "Nobody's wooing anyone, Mom. I think this one's woo-proof." He turns and winks at me, giving me a soft smile.

A few days ago I would've thought he was correct, but now...I'm just not sure. I think my stomach wants to prove him wrong though, because the butterflies are out in full force.

Amy laughs like she can't believe what she just heard. "Oh, honey. No one's woo-proof. We all like to be wooed."

"Dad!" Nate shouts as he fans the tomato slices out on the cutting board.

Jack appears in the doorway seconds later, wrapping one arm around Amy's waist. She places her hand atop his, and I find myself getting a little jealous of how cute they are. My parents could barely be in the same room together when they were married.

"Mom's talking about wooing again," he says, trying so hard to sound annoyed and failing miserably.

"He doesn't need your advice," Jack says, looking lovingly down at his wife. "He learned from the best."

Amy throws her head back, laughing. "You are an expert wooer."

"Someone please say 'woo' again," Nate says with mock exasperation.

"Woooooooooooo," Madeline yells as she runs past the kitchen door, and all four of us crack up.

"Let's leave them be," Jack says, gently pulling Amy away from the door.

"Clean up your mess, Nate." Amy winks at me before she takes Jack's hand and walks away.

"I love your family," I say, stealing a small piece of bacon from the plate on the stove. Is there anything more delicious than bacon? Answer: no.

"You wouldn't love them so much if you grew up with them." Nate's concentrating on spreading a layer of mayonnaise over a piece of toast.

I know he's just teasing me and I wouldn't expect anything else from him, but I want to tell him that growing up with them would've been better than growing up the way I did, with two parents who constantly screamed at each other until my father took off one day and never came back. But we're having such a good time together, and I want to keep things light. So I take a deep breath and swallow the words that are right on the tip of my tongue.

Nate looks over at me, a sad smile on his beautiful face. "I said the wrong thing, didn't I?"

I don't know how he always manages to see the things that I'm trying to hide.

"No." I shake my head, probably a little too quick of an answer to be believable. Still, I give him my best smile.

"Liar." He bumps his arm against mine, and god…his smile just lights me up inside.

I feel like I should reply, but I wait too long and by the time I think of something to say, there's been too much silence. It's too late. Nate seems to have moved on for now, concentrating on finishing our dinner. He walks over to the refrigerator and pulls out a container of potato salad that he says he made earlier. He cuts the sandwiches diagonally and puts two dollops of the potato salad on each plate. He puts sprigs of parsley on each plate, trying to make it look fancy. Surprisingly, he succeeds.

"I'm impressed," I tell him. Not that what he made is gourmet or anything, but because it's simple and it looks delicious.

"Sandwiches are a staple of mine. I'm also really good at ordering pizza."

He picks up the plates and I grab our drinks and we head out to a table on the back deck. Two sets of silverware are laying on pretty gingham napkins, and there are two jarred candles burning. I raise my eyebrow at him.

"It's citronella," he says quickly, defensively. "For mosquitoes."

I can't help the laugh that escapes me. "This seems kind of woo-y."

He looks at me, and there's something behind his eyes. Hope, maybe...I don't know. But whatever it is makes it difficult for me to look away. "I thought you couldn't be wooed."

"Your words, not mine." I shouldn't have said that, but a small part of me is glad that I did. In order to keep my mouth occupied before I slip up and say more things that I have no business saying, I take a bite of the sandwich, which is just...delicious. I try the potatoes, and they're awesome too. "You've perfected the BLT, Nate. And this potato salad is so good."

"I'm glad you like it," he says. "It's my grandmother's recipe."

"Really?" Even though I just watched him make the food that we're eating, I'm having difficulty reconciling this rugged man in front of me with the kind of person who talks about making potato salad from his grandmother's recipe. I picture him in his kitchen at home, wearing an apron and whipping up some recipe from his childhood. The thought of it makes me grin.

"What, you don't believe me?"

"I was just picturing you wearing an apron, that's all."

"I have one, you know," he says as he spears a few potatoes with his fork.

"Somehow that doesn't surprise me."

"It has 'Caution: Extremely Hot' written across the chest." He's completely serious, but he's smiling at me anyway.

I cover my mouth with my hand as I laugh, and his eyes linger on mine as my smile fades. Sometimes the way he looks at me is so intense that I'm not sure whether I should wrap my arms around him or run away.

"We should eat," he says, nodding towards my plate.

We slip into an easy silence through our meal, occasionally teasing, occasionally making small talk. It's not until we both finish that we have any semblance of a real conversation.

"That was the best sandwich I've ever had," I tell him as I fold up my napkin and place it on the table.

"Ever?" he asks, looking a little surprised and a lot pleased with himself.

"Well, my mom did make me this grilled cheese once...but that was a close second." I take a sip of wine and then lean back in my chair. "So, what do you do when you're not making BLTs?"

"I bought my first house a year ago," he says, pushing his plate away from him so there's room for him to rest his elbows on the table. "It's in a nice neighborhood and all, but it really needed some fixing up. I'm about halfway done now, but I spend a lot of my free time working on it. I recruit my friends to help me with the promise of free pizza and beer. I've become friendly with most of the people at Home Depot."

"And you've managed to stay out of the emergency room," I tease.

He laughs. "So far. When I'm not doing that, sometimes I head out to the lake near my house. I'll send a text to my buddies, and half the time we wind up hanging out there. We go swimming, drink a little. What about you?"

"My life is boring compared to yours."

"Doubtful. No home improvements to keep you busy?"

I shake my head. "I've been staying with my mom since the breakup. I intended for it to be temporary. I mean, it *is* temporary, I just haven't...you know." He's just going to let me keep rambling, so I make myself stop before he starts judging me or something. "I read a lot, do market research. I like to bake, although I haven't really been doing much of that lately. I work a lot. Like, *a lot* a lot." I shake my head and take another sip of wine. "God, I sound pathetic."

"No you don't. You sound like someone whose life changed and you just haven't caught up to it yet."

I grin because that's such a nice way of looking at it. I like the way Nate looks at life. I like the way he looks at *me*. "Thanks."

I reach back and pull my hair up off the back of my neck. It's a warm night—the warmest by far since I've been here—and I kind of want to go inside to get some relief.

"You know," Nate says, leaning toward me and resting his elbows on his knees. "Gabby and Ben aren't going to be back for hours. What do you have planned for the rest of the night?"

I shrug. "I don't know. Nothing yet."

With a mischievous glint in his eye, he asks, "Feel like going swimming?"

Chapter
ELEVEN

*T*he Wrights have an indoor pool, because Nate was right; this place really is a self-contained entertainment environment. The pool is fairly large, too, and I'm surprised I hadn't noticed it here before. It makes me wonder what else Amy and Jack have hidden in this house. A movie theater? A bowling alley? I want to ask, but I'm afraid that the words would come out wrong, like I'm somehow making fun of their wealth. So I keep my mouth shut.

There are dim lights along the walls next to the windows, and the lights inside the pool are dim, too. The low lighting creates a romantic type of atmosphere that I'm not entirely sure that I'm comfortable with, and that's not because I don't want to get romantic with Nate, but more because I do. The more I'm around him, the more I want it. And that's dangerous, that's bad. That's everything I promised myself I wouldn't do, especially if I'm going to make it out of the next four days unscathed. I can enjoy myself when I'm with him, I just can't let myself get in too deep.

"I like your suit," he says, offering me a mischievous grin. Again, it's like he knows what I'm thinking and wants me to stop thinking so much.

I look down at my simple red bikini, as if I've forgotten what it is that I'm wearing. "Thanks," I tell him. "I like yours too."

They're blue swim trunks, nothing really special. But they hang low on his waist, and because he doesn't have a shirt on I can ogle his abs, which are... incredible. I want to tell him that, but I don't.

Nate quickly looks down, as if he's forgotten what he was wearing too.

"You're lucky I decided to forego the banana hammock for you today."

I laugh. "I appreciate that." Although I'm sure if anyone can make that look good, it's him.

The water in the pool is very warm, and Nate and I are standing together in the shallow end, the water close to our knees. I take a few steps forward and he follows suit, until we're waist-deep. I skim my fingers across the surface of the water, enjoying the soft feel of it on my fingertips. It's been a long time since I've been in a pool, and this memory of my father and me swimming pops into my mind. Unlike most of the other memories I have of him, this one makes me smile.

"What are you thinking about?" Nate asks.

"My dad," I tell him, not even stopping to think about whether sharing this would be a good idea. About whether I even want to. It seems my mouth has made up its mind for me. I want him to know, although I'm not sure why. "We used to go swimming a lot when I was a kid," I say. Nate's looking at me like I'm telling the most interesting story he's ever heard, which encourages me to continue. "He used to do this thing where he'd crouch down in the water and I'd put my feet on his shoulders. He'd grip my ankles and then he'd pop up and throw me across the pool. It was fun."

Nate smiles. I get the feeling that he's glad I shared with him, but I can also tell he knows exactly what I'm talking about.

"Madeline likes to do that too."

"A girl after my own heart."

A few seconds later, Nate dives into the water and swims into the deep end, about ten feet away from me. When he comes up, he treads water.

"You should come down this way," he says. "The water's clear, so you can see we don't have an eel infestation."

I bring my hand up to rub the back of my neck. It's so difficult for me to stay away from him, especially with the promise of his wet skin just waiting for me at the other end of the pool. I want to put my hands all over him, it's almost like a sickness how badly I want it.

"Are you afraid of getting your hair wet?"

"No!" I yell, half laughing. Just to show him how not afraid to get my hair wet I am, I dive under the water and swim over, giving his foot a gentle tug before I surface right in front of him, so we're facing each other.

"You look good," he says, giving me one of those smiles that makes me feel like my heart tripped and flipped and fell on its ass.

"You are so smooth."

"I'm not trying to be smooth. I mean it."

I roll my eyes.

"Why can't I just give you a compliment?" he asks.

I look at him for a long while, and I don't know that I have an answer for him. I swim over to the side of the pool, because suddenly my heart feels so heavy that I'm not sure I can stay afloat anymore. Nate follows.

"Callie," he says, very softly.

My back is pressed against the shiny blue tiles that line the perimeter, and I'm looking down at my hands, all distorted by the water. He grips the concrete edge of the pool, one hand on either side of my head. He's got me boxed in, but I don't feel threatened by it. He's close, but I could swim away if I wanted to.

The thing is, I don't want to.

"He really did a number on you, didn't he?" Nate says, not even trying to hide his anger. "You're still torn up over it." And the way the words come out, they're a statement of fact. I have to set the record straight.

"I'm not torn up over it," I tell him, looking him right in the eyes. And that's the truth. I mean, it's part of the truth, but things aren't that simple.

"Callie-"

"I'm not. See, the thing is that I thought this would be us, you know? Me and Ethan getting married. Having a wedding, spending the rest of our lives together. I thought that's where we were headed. I let myself believe I had forever with him, and then I came home and found him in bed with another woman. In *our* bed. And I just...I couldn't believe it."

"Cheating isn't usually about the sex," he says, like that matters at all.

"That doesn't make it any better, Nate. That makes it worse."

He nods, looking down, and I'm not sure if he doesn't say anything because he wants me to keep going or because he just doesn't know what else to say. There's a part of me that's ready to say this, to admit it out loud, and I want to admit it to him.

"Six months later, it's not the sex that bothers me. Well, not really. It's that I never thought he could do something like that to me. I didn't think he was even capable of it. I was supposed to be the person who knew him better than anyone else, and I wonder how deep would I have gotten before I found out? Would we have gotten married? Would we have had children? How long would it have taken me to figure out that I didn't know him at all? That's what scares the hell out of me. So it's not about him, you know? It's about me. I don't trust myself to know who it's safe to give my heart to."

Nate takes a deep breath, and his face is so full of understanding that I could cry. He reaches up and pushes a strand of hair behind my ear, and his expression is so tender that I can't help but press my cheek into the palm of his hand and close my eyes. He makes me feel safe, and I don't know if it's right, but I want to allow myself the comfort that he offers, even though that's so dangerous. It would be so easy for me to let myself fall in love with him. So easy to let him in. So easy for him to break my heart.

Nate's hand slides down the side of my neck, and he traces the strap of my swimsuit with his fingertip. I can feel the trail of heat his touch leaves all the way down in my toes. "You won't ever know who it's safe to give your heart to. Falling in love is a risk."

I laugh bitterly. "I think it's well documented that I'm not much of a risk taker."

He smiles, putting his hand back on the edge of the pool. "Not every guy is like Ethan."

I know he's dying to tell me that *he* isn't like Ethan, but he doesn't do that. I don't know why his silence makes me believe him more than his words ever could, but everything in my brain is just a big swirl of confusion right now.

"But some guys are, Nate. How will I know the difference?"

He waits for me to look into his eyes before he speaks. "You'll feel it."

He says the words with conviction, and I want to believe him. I do know that I feel *something* when I'm with him, and I'm not sure whether it's something I can't name or something I just don't want to name. Whatever it is though, it's driving me crazy; it's making me want to run in ten directions at once.

Nate's leg brushes against mine, and all of a sudden I can feel his chest pressing against me. I'm not sure if he moved closer or if I did, but that doesn't really matter anyway. I move my leg so that my foot presses up against the wall behind me because I need some leverage, and as I'm moving my thigh brushes up against his erection. He inhales a sharp, quick breath at the contact, looking at me with intensity behind his eyes that sends a nervous rush through me. And the truth is that I'm so tired of trying to sort out these feelings. I want Nate to feel; I want to be taken out of the equation, just for a little while.

Before I can talk myself out of all the reasons why this is a very bad idea, I wrap my legs around the backs of Nate's thighs in order to hold myself up. I slide my hand across his shoulder and wrap my arm around his neck, then slide my other hand down his chest, gently grazing his skin with my fingernails. The contact makes his eyelids flutter. He reaches up to touch my face, but when I look at him, he knows that I need him to let me drive this. He knows that I need him to just put his hand back on the side of the pool. So, he does.

I want to kiss him so badly, but if I do I know I'll never stop. I'll get so lost that I don't know if I'll ever be able to find my way back again. I'm not sure that I'd want to, and that scares the hell out of me.

I run my fingertips along the waistband of Nate's swim trunks, and his muscles contract beneath my touch. I like teasing him, making him wait. But I'm not doing this to be cruel, so it's not long before I slip my hand below the fabric and glide my palm along the length of his erection. I clasp my hand around him and slide it down. Nate's head rolls to the side, his perfect, stubbly jaw on offer for my kisses. I press my lips there, then gently nip at his chin, drawing a low kind of growl from him that spurs me on. I take another pass downward and he bucks his hips into my hand, needing more friction. His breath quickens as I move, and my eyes meet his. He tilts his head and moves forward just a bit, wanting to kiss me, but I look down because I can't let myself do that right now. I focus my attention on what I'm doing, and when my thumb skims over the tip of Nate's dick, his eyes squeeze shut. The water makes everything more sensitive for me, so I can imagine how much better this feels for him.

"Callie," he says, whispering my name. He presses his forehead against mine, and I can feel the warmth of his breath on my cheek. His lips are right there, and I manage to have the willpower to not taste him. I manage to go against every instinct that's coursing through my body, and somehow this—touching him like this and not kissing him—is the sexiest thing I've ever done.

Still stroking him, I slide my other hand up the back of his neck and lightly scratch my nails against along his scalp. I remember that he liked it the first night we were together in Dallas, and he likes it now. I can tell by the way his breathing picks up and his muscles loosen. It's like he can't hold his head up anymore and he brings it to rest on my shoulder as I push him higher and higher.

"Nate, are you in here?"

Shit—it's Jessa.

His name echoes throughout the room, and his head snaps back in an instant. I pull my hand away from him and duck under his arm. Jessa walks over right as I'm pulling myself up onto the pool deck, and I'm thankful she had the foresight to call out his name before she walked in here.

"Hey Callie," she says, offering me a smile.

I smile back at her as I pick up a towel and wrap it around myself. My heart is pounding so hard in my chest that I can practically see it thrumming beneath my skin. "Hey," I reply, pushing back the growing wave of disappointment that Nate and I were interrupted.

"What's up?" Nate asks. His voice is kind of gravely; it's huskier than usual. I wonder if Jessa notices the difference.

"Mom was looking for you, she wanted you to help her move some tables. I'll just tell her you're busy."

"It's okay," I tell her. "I was just going to head back to my room. I'm feeling a little tired."

Nate sighs. "I'll be right there."

Jessa walks out, and I tug the towel tighter around me as I look over at Nate. His arms are crossed on the side of the pool, his forehead pressed against his arm, looking down. Maybe I should say something, but I don't. I just turn and walk away.

Chapter TWELVE

*W*hile Nate and I were having dinner, Amy moved my things into the last spare bedroom that was available in the main house. It just so happens to be right at the beginning of the hallway that leads to Nate's room. I'd only spent a few minutes in here earlier when I changed into my swimsuit, and honestly, I don't really want to be in here right now. I want to be back at the pool with Nate. I regret leaving the way that I did; I regretted it the second that I walked away.

I reek of chlorine, and every time I smell it I remember the way Nate looked at me when I was touching him. Those kinds of memories make it impossible for me to think straight, so I walk into the bathroom and turn on the faucet. Once the water is hot enough, I strip off my suit and step into the shower.

Under the warm, relaxing water, my mind drifts back to Nate, to what we just did. Or what *I* just did, I guess. I don't know why I feel so drawn to him; it's completely ridiculous. I've known him less than a week. The thing is, I love talking to him and being around him. It's stupid for me to try to ignore that, isn't it? But when I'm around him, I just want to kiss him. I want to talk to him for hours. I want to wake up with him, I want to share my bed with him. I remember feeling the same way with Ethan, even though those things didn't come nearly as quickly.

Nate was right, not everyone is like Ethan. Maybe Nate wouldn't cheat on me, but maybe he'd leave like my dad did. Or maybe things just wouldn't work out between us for whatever reason. That would hurt just as much.

This is the reason that women like me aren't cut out for one-night stands. I can't separate the feelings from the sex, even with a stranger. And I tell myself that this isn't a *stranger*, this is Nate. I wouldn't be feeling this way if he hadn't shown up at this wedding though, would I? Maybe I could've just gone on with my life and let the sex be sex, even though I did have difficulty leaving him the morning after. Ugh, this is maddening.

I just want to turn off my brain and have fun. Why is that so difficult for me? He flat-out told me that I could use him for his body, and I know he wasn't kidding, so it's not like he's averse to the idea. What's so wrong with me enjoying his company while he's here? Even if I do have feelings, what can even become of them? On Sunday we'll leave. He'll go back to Colorado and I'll go back to Texas. A long-distance thing wouldn't ever work between us. And there can't be heartbreak waiting for me on the other side of something I knew wouldn't work out anyway, right?

I'm young, and I should be out in the world having fun. I know that when I leave here I'll regret keeping him at arm's length more than I'll ever regret him being closer, especially since shutting him out means I'm missing out on a good time with a great guy, however short that good time may be. I can't keep having this argument with myself; it's a waste of time and energy.

When the water starts to cool, I turn off the shower, towel dry my hair, and put on my pajamas. I feel like I need to make a peace offering to Nate for running out on him earlier, and I have the perfect idea. I sit down on my bed and fire up my laptop, then pull up Photoshop, more inspired than I've been in years. It doesn't take me long to work up a few draft logos based on what he told me about his start-up company last night. When I'm satisfied with the few samples that I have, I work up the courage to walk down the hall to his room.

I stand in the middle of the hallway between Nate's room and mine, staring at the rectangle of light that streams across the shiny wooden floor. Nate's door is open, like he hoped that I was going to walk in. Maybe he knew that I would want to, I'm not sure. He seems to understand some things about me that I haven't quite gotten a handle on myself, and it's both disconcerting and wonderful at the same time. It's nice to have someone around who instinctively knows what you need.

Quietly drumming my fingertips along the edge of my laptop, which is tucked under my arm, I take the few steps forward until I can peer inside his room. He's sitting on the floor, his back resting against the bed. His right leg is hiked up, the other one stretched out in front of him. His his elbow is resting on his knee, and he's holding a book. He's intent on what he's reading. I can't make out the title of the book, but it's thick and dog-eared, like he's read it a hundred times. Some passage is making him smile, and the temptation to just stand there and watch him is overwhelming. In order to keep my creepy level as low as possible, I knock on the doorframe so that he knows I'm standing here.

Nate's head snaps up, and he looks at me like I'm the only person in the world that he wants to see. His eyes dart down to the laptop that's cradled under my arm, but then he smiles at me and all of a sudden I can't remember why I was nervous to come to see him.

"Hey," he says, closing the book and laying it on the floor beside him.

"Hey. Mind if I come in?"

"Never." He moves to his right a little, even though there's plenty of room on the floor for me already. He pats the spot next to him and I walk over and lay my laptop on the bed, then fold my legs under me and sit down.

I owe him an apology, and for whatever reason, it doesn't come easy. I wring my hands together, my fingers practically white at the knuckles until Nate places his hand on top of mine. The second his skin touches my skin, all the tension in my body just melts away. Even though he knows I have something to say, he doesn't press me for it; he just gives me all the time I need.

I take a deep breath and exhale slowly. "I'm really sorry that I left the way that I did earlier."

He lets out a little laugh. "It's not like we could've kept going."

"No, but I could've stayed. I just-"

"It's okay."

Finally, I turn my head and look over at him. His eyes are clear, his expression soft, and the smile on his face is genuine. I get lost in that smile for a beat longer than I should before I make myself turn away. Looking at the floor in front of me, I notice all the photographs scattered there. Next to them is a photo album, opened to a page somewhere in the middle.

"What's this?" I ask, leaning forward and plucking a photo out of the pile. It's a picture of Ben and Nate, and it has to be at least ten years old. They both look nearly identical, only their faces are less angular, still softened by the early adolescent pudge they hadn't quite lost yet. The two of them are standing in the middle of what must be a forest clearing, arms slung around each other's shoulders. They're both wearing white tees with *The Wright Stuff* written across the chest. Try as I might, I can't help but laugh. "What are these shirts?"

Nate shakes his head like he knew this was coming, but he doesn't really look all that embarrassed and there's something about it that's endearing. "That was taken at some family reunion. That year was the Wright family reunion, so the theme was The Wright Stuff. Of course we had to have shirts. Mom's also really big on the mister Wright with a 'W'-slash-mister right with an 'R' comparisons, just so you can prepare yourself for that when she gives her toast at the wedding on Saturday."

"I'm looking forward to it," I say. I don't dare tell him that I think those t-shirts were kind of adorable. "So you were just feeling nostalgic tonight?"

"Mom wanted me to find some pictures of Ben and me as kids so she could put them up on this cork board she's going to have at the reception. This should be sufficiently embarrassing for him."

"I think it's cute," I say, trailing my fingertip along the edge of the photograph. "And you were cute."

"Were?" Nate asks, teasing.

I shrug. "I don't know that I'd describe you as cute now."

"What would you describe me as?"

I feel the blush creep up my neck into my cheeks, and avoid looking at him by averting my attention to a stack of photos to the right of the album. I pick it up and flip through the pictures one by one. They're all of Nate in his ridiculously gorgeous outdoorsy glory. Camping, waterskiing. Snowboarding. It's not until I'm halfway through the pile that I come across one of him with a woman. She's got bright blonde sun-kissed hair, and her cheeks are rosy from the cold air. The two of them are standing in front of a beige tent, and there's a beautiful crystal-blue lake in the background. Nate is kissing this woman, the kind of kiss where you can see them smiling even though their lips are pressed together, and I take a deep breath to push down the tide of jealousy that I feel rising inside of me.

"Was she your girlfriend?" I ask, tilting my head up to look at him.

He nods. "Caroline. We dated in college."

"What happened?" I ask, not even stopping to think about how it really isn't any of my business. "I'm sorry, I shouldn't have asked that."

Nate grins. It's a sweet kind of smile; one that I haven't seen on him before. "It's okay. We graduated from college and she moved to Connecticut for a job. We tried to make it work for a couple of months, but it was the kind of relationship that thrived on keggers and weekend retreats. Not that great in real life."

I crinkle my brow, kind of surprised that he's being so honest. "Was she your last girlfriend?"

He laughs. "No, there have been a few since."

"A few?" I shouldn't be surprised, I don't even know why I am. Look at him, I mean…how could he be single for long?

"Mercy, Jane and Rachel. One was long term, and the other two, well…not so much."

"They couldn't handle your charm?" I tease, bumping his shoulder with mine.

Nate takes a deep breath. "Rachel couldn't handle me leaving the cap off the toothpaste and leaving crumbs on the counter after I made a sandwich. Neither of which I do anymore, for the record," he says. "Jane couldn't handle the fact that I was not, and could not ever be just like her ex-boyfriend. He was perfect, apparently. She made sure to tell me that often. Mercy and I, we just didn't fit."

"That's a nice way of putting it," I tell him, fiddling with the hem of my shirt. "I should start telling everyone that Ethan and I just didn't fit, instead of, you know, telling them what happened."

Nate shrugs. "It's the truth though, regardless of what got you to the not fitting part of things."

"And you just keep trying? Keep putting yourself out there?" The idea of moving from potential broken heart to potential broken heart just astounds me. I can't wrap my brain around it.

"I'm not going to find the woman who fits unless I date a few who don't."

"And what if no one fits?" It hurts a little to say the words aloud, although I know that's because this is my fear. I don't think Nate worries about being alone for the rest of his life.

"That would suck," he says, his blue eyes locked with mine. "But at least I'd be able to say that I tried. It seems like a lonely life, not trying."

"It's a heartbreak-free life."

"True, but what's the good without the bad?"

He has a point, and even though I really wish I could argue with it, I can't. I admire the positivity in his outlook on life, but I know it comes from a place deep inside of him that's firmly rooted in positivity based on the way he grew up. His sister is married, and his brother is getting married in a few days. His parents have been together forever. For someone like me, relationship positivity isn't so easy to come by. I didn't grow up the same way he did.

"It seems like a lot of people in your family have found their fit," I tell him.

"And a lot of people in yours haven't." He just knows, not that it'd be all that difficult to figure out.

I laugh, but it's short and bitter, and I don't like the way it makes Nate look at me, like he's half concerned and way too curious. Like he's finally able to piece together the parts of my life that hadn't been making sense to him before.

"That's an understatement," I tell him, trying like hell to sound cheerful. But I don't really want to get into this right now, so I look down at the pictures that I'm still holding. I flip through a few more, and this set is just of Nate, no Caroline. He's skiing in one, and jumping off a cliff into a lake in another. "You really do jump off cliffs, don't you?"

He smiles and shrugs. "Sometimes."

"You like the feeling of falling?"

"There's nothing else in the world like it," he replies, his eyes so bright and intense and full of meaning. Meaning that I can't quite figure out. "I climb things too, just so you know."

"So you can rappel off of them. Crazy."

"There are some things that are so beautiful that you can only see them if you climb to the top of a mountain. Or jump off a cliff."

There's that positivity, just pulling me to him like a magnet. All of his hope and lightheartedness and kindness of spirit are combining with his beautiful face and body to be the absolute death of me. I wish I could give in to it for good, to see where this could go. But I've known him for less than a week. I have to keep reminding myself that it's easy to make people see what you want them to see when you only have to do it for a little while. How can I know if I'm seeing the real him?

I look up into his eyes, steely blue and focused right on me. "I can't imagine what that would be."

A small grin pulls at his lips, drawing my gaze there, and god, I really want to put my mouth on his. I want to get lost in the feel of his stubble against my cheek, and his hands cradling the back of my head as he kisses me. But I'm scared to do that, because I know that a kiss will be more than a kiss between him and me.

"Speaking of jumping," I say, desperate to change the subject. My voice is a little hazy, but I reach over and grab my laptop, flipping open the screen while I give myself a few seconds to regroup. "I want to show you something." I open the Rocky Mountain Rec logos I drafted earlier, and line them up on my screen so he can see all of them at once. "I've been thinking about this ever since our conversation last night. I hope you don't mind."

I tilt the laptop so that Nate can see the screen, and the look on his face is indescribable. Part happiness, part shock, part something else that I can't quite identify. Maybe it's got something to do with my show of support when his own father isn't really keen on the idea of him and his friend starting their own business. Maybe it's just nice for him to know that someone's behind him. Either way, I like his smile. I like the way the laptop brightens his face.

"You designed these?" Nate asks, his voice incredulous as he leans down to get a closer look at the screen.

"Yeah. I just got a few ideas in my head and I went with them. You don't have to use them or anything, but I thought-"

"Callie." He interrupts me, his voice so soft. He puts his hand on top of mine and gives it a squeeze, and the warmth of his skin makes my eyelids flutter. "Thank you."

I smile. "You're welcome."

He takes a while to study each one, and when he lets go of my hand, I miss the feel of him immediately. "See," he says, pointing to the first of the four designs I showed him. "*This* is a groundbreaking font choice."

I let out a genuine laugh, my head tilting back to rest against his bed. "Thanks."

He turns to me, his eyes hooded. He licks his perfect lips, and he's looking at me like he wants to kiss me. I'm looking at him like I want him to, I know it. But for whatever reason, I shy away. Stupid brain. Stupid broken heart.

"I should probably go," I whisper. "It's getting late."

Nate presses his lips together in a thin line, then inhales a deep breath through his nose. He closes my laptop and reluctantly hands it to me. I take it and stand.

"Thank you," he says, his voice tight.

I nod, smiling.

I walk down the hallway feeling like I left a piece of myself back there in his room. Only an hour ago I had decided to stop thinking so much and just let myself have a little fun. Then he had to go and talk about girlfriends and commitment, and I talked myself right back into denying him. Why can't I just let him kiss me? It's a kiss, it feels good. What's so wrong with feeling good? I reach up and touch my lips, remembering the heat of his mouth that night in the hotel room. I want to feel that heat again. What am I doing? Why do I keep letting myself walk away from him when I just want to…I want…

A kiss. Just one kiss.

Before I can talk myself out of it, I put my laptop on my bed and run my fingers through my hair. I retrace the steps I just took, back to Nate's room, where the door is still open. He's standing beside his bed, leaning over and pulling back the sheets. He stills the second I reach the doorway, like he can feel my presence. Maybe he's as attuned to me as I am to him.

When his eyes meet mine, I'm drawn across the room like I'm on autopilot, like I don't have any choice in the matter. And then I'm right in front of him, and he's looking at me like he can see through all of my fears and all of my excuses. Like he sees right down into the heart of me. And the thing is, I can't look away. The light hits his eyes in a way that makes them *so* blue. His pupils are rimmed in a darker color, and I think his eyes are the most beautiful thing I've ever seen in my life.

Without thinking, I reach up and skim my fingers across his brow bone and down his temple to his cheeks. His eyelids flutter shut and he licks his lips and my heart his pounding so hard that I know he must be able to feel it through my fingertips. He turns his head a little, and his quickening breaths slip across my wrist, and then those gorgeous eyes are on mine again. My fingers slip back along the column of his neck as my other hand slides up his chest and around his shoulder. I pull myself up onto my tiptoes and press my lips against his before I lose my nerve. Instantly, one of Nate's hands makes its way along my waist, coming to rest on the small of my back, pulling me against his body. The other threads into my hair, cradling my head as my knees turn to jelly.

Kissing him feels as easy and necessary as breathing. He tastes like I remember, his tongue so perfect against mine, and he makes these soft noises as we move together that I want to keep for the rest of my life. I want to be the only one who ever gets to hear them.

We kiss like we're never going to stop, for minutes or maybe hours. However long it is it's not enough, and when we finally part, I feel lost. Nate presses his forehead against mine, and I trace his neck and shoulders with my fingers. He closes his eyes and sighs, then crooks his finger beneath my chin and lifts my head until our lips meet again in a slower, more tender kiss.

When we break apart this time, I slide my hands down his arms, letting our fingers tangle together before I pull away. I want more, but if I'm going to allow myself to have this until we leave, I need to know that I can control it. I need to know that this can be on my own terms.

"Callie," Nate whispers.

There are so many things I want to say to him, want to do with him. I promised myself one kiss, but I took two.

"Goodnight," I say quietly, offering him a smile. It's a genuine one, full of all the things I can't say.

It takes everything I have in me to walk out the door.

Chapter
THIRTEEN

*T*he Wrights' backyard is decorated with colorful hanging lanterns; blue, red, purple and yellow globes casting soft light across the yard as they dangle from wires stretched between trees. The rest of the very small bridal party arrived earlier this afternoon, and Amy is celebrating all of us finally being in one place by throwing a pre-rehearsal dinner dinner. We've kind of naturally gravitated into two groups, divided by sex. Gabby and I are sitting with two of our dearest friends, both of whom are here to be bridesmaids in the wedding. There's Jasmine, with her ebony skin and long, sleek hair and smile that can make you spill your deepest, darkest secrets, and Shelby, the shy, bookish brunette with a wild streak in her that you'd never see coming. Ethan's Emily sits on the perimeter of our little circle; not quite part of the group, not quite a stranger.

"Morocco or Greece, those are your choices?" Gabby asks, looking at Jasmine like her potential vacation destinations are the worst places to visit in the entire world.

"I know that's not judgment I hear, Gabby Morgan." Jasmine is using that voice she reserves for the times when she wants you to know that she's just not going to take any of your shit anymore.

"It's just…why go alone? On a trip like that?" Gabby asks.

"Because I want to go on a vacation, and I'm not going to sit around waiting for some man to take me."

"You sound like Callie," Gabby says.

"Hey," I reply, with not entirely mock offense. "Leave me out of this."

"If Callie wants to be man-free, I support that," Jasmine says, smiling at me. "I work hard. I'm married to my job. Healthiest relationship I've ever had, truthfully. I got a promotion, so I'm taking myself on a celebratory trip. My own personal honeymoon, if you will," she says before taking a sip from the glass of wine she's holding in her right hand. "And I won't have to pick up after some slob."

"A honeymoon without the sex," Shelby reminds her. Shelby's level of pervertedness could put a man to shame.

"Girl, I can get the sex without the commitment." Jasmine smirks in Shelby's direction. "I'll meet some Greek hottie and get myself all taken care of. You two can marry off if you want to," she says, waving her hand dismissively at Gabby and Shelby. "I'm happy by myself."

I sigh, wishing I could be that sure about my life of self-imposed solitude. I'm doing it more out of necessity than preference. I don't want a broken heart; Jasmine doesn't want a commitment. Jasmine comes and sits down next to me, and when I turn my head to smile at her, I catch a glimpse of Nate. Nate, Ben, and their father are over on the patio of the guest house, standing around the grill, beers in hand. Marco and Xavier, Ben's groomsmen are there too, animatedly talking to Mr. Wright, probably discussing the proper torque in a '67 Mustang or whatever it is that men talk about when they're being all manly. Nate looks up at the same time I do, and our eyes meet. He smiles, nodding toward me, and I smile back, a warm rush of nerves tingling all the way down to my toes. Even standing all the way across the yard, he still knows how to get to me.

"Ben's brother's testing your vow of celibacy, isn't he?" Jasmine says softly, so that I'm the only one who can hear her. "I know that look, Callie. You're in trouble already and you don't even know it."

I grin, because she's wrong, wrong, wrong. I'm in trouble, sure. But I definitely know it.

"So, Emily," Shelby says, and I feel this sense of dread creeping up inside of me, spreading its icy fingers across my belly. Gabby and I both told Shelby and Jasmine of the Ethan-slash-Emily situation and drilled into them that talk of my history with Ethan is forbidden, but they've both got some alcohol in them, so who knows what'll happen? "How did you meet Ethan?"

I give Shelby a dirty look, but she completely ignores me. I'm not really all that upset about it, because honestly, I want to hear Emily's answer.

Emily looks across the yard at Ethan, smiling before she answers. "We met at a karaoke bar."

Jasmine nearly spits out her drink.

"A karaoke bar?" I ask, completely confused. Ethan loathes karaoke. Or, I guess, he used to.

"Yeah. It was a friend's birthday party. We bonded over the fact that we were the only two who refused to sing."

It's ridiculous, but there's a part of me that's relieved to know that I was right about the karaoke.

"How long have you been together?" I ask. Gabby glares at me, but I don't care. She can be surprised all she wants. I'm going to break my own rules tonight, because I just *have* to know the answer.

"A couple of months," she says, pushing a strand of hair behind her ear. She's such a pretty woman, and there's something about her that's so bright, like she just exudes light. I can see why Ethan would be drawn to her.

"What do you do?" Jasmine asks.

"I'm a speech therapist at an elementary school in Fort Worth."

"She also paints in her spare time," Gabby says, chiming in. She says it with such enthusiasm that I wonder if she's just been biding her time, hoping my curiosity would pique so that I'd start asking her questions like these.

I wait a few beats before I say something. "What do you paint?"

"Landscapes, mostly."

"Show her," Gabby says, nudging Emily's shoulder.

Reluctantly, Emily fishes her phone out of her back pocket and she scrolls through a few photos before she hands the phone to me.

When I see the paintings, I'm stunned. They're remarkably beautiful even with the cell phone's awful picture quality. Breathtaking, really. It's difficult for me to believe that someone I've actually met has painted them, which I know is ridiculous.

"Emily," I say, smiling at her. "These are gorgeous."

"Thank you," she says. I can see her blush even under the dim lantern light.

I return her phone to her, and for the first time all night, it seems like none of us have anything to say.

"Can I ask you all a question that I've been wondering about all afternoon?" Emily asks, seeming kind of shy. She stands up and takes a seat next to Jasmine, then leans in. I don't know who she thinks will overhear her, the guys are at least 30 yards away. "That guy over there," she says, pointing towards the men gathered around the grill. "The one in the red shirt?"

"That's Marco," Shelby says.

"Yeah, him. Why does he have a tattoo of a Ring Pop?"

We all bust out laughing, clutching our stomachs, gasping for air. Jasmine's having the most difficulty catching her breath, because she's been harassing Marco about that tattoo ever since he got it, and I know she's got to feel validated right now.

"Marco!" she shouts.

Every single head turns in our direction and Marco yells, "What?"

"Emily here wants to know all about your Ring Pop tattoo."

Marco's shoulders slump as Xavier, Ethan and Ben all crack up.

"It's an *ankh*, you assholes!" he yells.

Emily shakes her head, grinning. "It's a Ring Pop," she says under her breath.

God help me, I like her.

"*T*his is the best hamburger I think I've ever had," Shelby says, tilting her head to lick a piece of melted cheese that's dripping off of her thumb.

I hum in agreement, remembering that my dad used to tell me that the messier the food, the better it tastes. The memory stirs up an unexpected warmth inside of me, and I tamp it down as soon as it rises up. Memories of my father are seldom good things, and when they are they usually leave as quickly as they came.

"We bought it from just down the street," Jessa says, and every single member of the Wright family groans, Gabby included.

"I don't want to think about my food having a face, Jess." Nate looks warily down at his hamburger, but keeps eating it anyway.

Jessa rolls her eyes. "You always were really sensitive about animals."

"Not to the point where he won't eat them," Marco replies. "He pounded down about fifty sliders at Ben's bachelor party."

"What happens in Vegas," Nate says before taking another bite.

"You went veggie for a while when you were like, ten, right?" Jessa asks.

"Please don't tell that story right now." Nate puts his burger down and wipes his hands on the crumpled-up paper towel in front of him.

"What story?" I ask, figuring out that if Nate doesn't want it told, it must definitely be worth hearing. He rolls his eyes at me, but follows it up with a cute grin.

"Mom, you wanna take this one?" Jessa picks up her bottle of beer and swirls it before taking a sip.

"Back before we built the patio onto the guest house," Amy begins, smiling, "there was a huge tree back there, and we had a problem with baby birds and squirrels falling off of the branches. Nate always used to watch out for them, and when one of them would fall, he'd build them a little bed by filling a shoe box with old dishtowels. He'd feed them with ear droppers until they were big enough to go out on their own again."

Nate looks completely embarrassed, and a few of the guys at the table are doing their best not to laugh at him, which is probably in their own best interest, because Nate could definitely take all of them. At once, probably. I can tell that Ethan wants to make a crack, and there's a part of me that wants to see what would no doubt be a smack down of epic proportions on Nate's behalf. But Ethan decides not to take the bait. The women, well...every one of them but those in his immediate family is looking at him all starry eyed and I'm a little jealous about it, honestly. There's a part of me that wants to walk over to where he's sitting, stand in front of him and write MINE all over his plain grey t-shirt. But that's crazy, isn't it? Wanting to mark my territory when there's no territory to mark? I can't have Nate-ish territory.

Right?

What is *wrong* with me?

Thankfully, Nate seems to be oblivious to his adoring female audience. "Can we talk about anything other than my wildlife rescue hospital?"

Amy sighs when she looks at her son, her hands clasped in front of her. In no time at all she's turned her attention to Xavier.

"How's your mama?" she asks. Xavier's mom was diagnosed with breast cancer a few years ago. She's doing well now, but for a while there…

"She's great, thank you for asking," he says, his mouth half-full. He smiles at her, and this cute dimple makes a dent in his cheek. It makes me remember why I had a slight crush on him when I first met him all those years ago.

"She'd smack you if she saw you talking with food in your mouth," Jasmine says in a half-biting, half-sweet kind of tone. She and Xavier dated in high school, back before any of us knew them. They broke up the summer before college, but Jasmine teases him a little too much, and Xavier always looks at her a beat longer than he probably should. There's something there still, but I don't think they'll ever act on it, and what kind of hypocrite would I be if I called either one of them out?

"It wouldn't be the first time," Ben says.

Amy rolls her eyes at her son, but she smiles in spite of herself. "Marco, how's everything with you?"

"Well, thank you." He's always so polite.

"Since we've got a wedding coming up and I've got brides on my mind, I have to ask. Have you proposed to that girlfriend of yours yet?"

Marco's mid-swallow, and he nearly chokes on his food. Ben gives him a light pat on the back, but it doesn't take Marco long to recover.

"No, ma'am. I haven't."

"Well, what are you waiting for?" Amy asks.

Marco shrugs, and his face gets serious all of a sudden as he looks around the table, like he doesn't know how to answer her. "I'm not sure if she's the one."

"Ah," Amy sighs. "It's best to wait then."

"How do you know?" Shelby asks. "When somebody's 'the one?'"

"I knew when Jack flew across the Atlantic from Paris to Philly while he was still studying abroad, just so that we could be together on Christmas," Amy says, and unlike the other night at dinner, not a single one of her children playfully groan at this story.

Jack chimes in, taking hold of Amy's hand. "And I knew when she spent her entire Christmas break trying to mend me back to health."

This sweet, almost bashful smile pulls at Jessa's lips. "I knew when Ryan was the first person I wanted to call whenever something good happened. Or when I just wanted to tell someone about my day."

I look over at Ethan, and his eyes meet mine. There's a sadness behind them, and I'm wondering if he's thinking the same thing that I am. He was never—not once during the course of our relationship—that person for me. I always called Gabby with good news, or whenever I wanted to talk.

Gabby's got this distant look in her eyes. "Ben and I went away for a long weekend in Austin," she says, looking over at him. "We had tickets for this play that I'd been wanting to see forever." What she doesn't say is that she'd had an aversion to going to the theater ever since her parents died, and that weekend was a big step for her. But she doesn't need to tell the people at this table that, everyone who she cares about knowing the story already knows it. "It was really important to me that I wear this bracelet that belonged to my mother. But I was so nervous that somehow I managed to leave it behind. It seems so trivial, this piece of jewelry, but there was a story behind it, and I just…I needed to wear it that night." She smiles at Ben with unshed tears in her eyes, and he's watching her like she's the most precious thing in his world. "Ben drove all the way back to Dallas to get it, just so I could wear it. That's when I knew."

She touches Ben's cheek and leans in for a kiss.

"Usually Ben's the forgetful one," Amy says.

"Like how he forgot the wedding rings." Jessa's eyes widen, and she slams her palm against her mouth when she realizes she let something slip that she shouldn't have.

"Relax," Ben says, stroking the back of Gabby's hand. "Nate picked them up on his way out here."

"And then he missed his flight because he stopped to get barbecue and got stuck in traffic," Jessa says, and my stomach just…drops.

But there was a weather delay that night. He told me he couldn't get a flight out until the next morning.

Nate looks over at me, his eyes wide and uncertain. The words his sister just said replay on a loop in my brain.

*I*t's well past one in the morning when everyone finally begins to shuffle off to their rooms, tired from a long night of eating and laughter and fun between friends. Even though I haven't known most of the Wright family for long, and I haven't spent any quality time with my friends in the bridal party for a while, there was something very homey and familiar about this evening that makes the end of it bittersweet.

I'm not very tired, and it seems that Nate's still wide awake, too. I have a feeling that he's just waiting to get me alone so that he can explain the whole airport story that Jessa let slip. I can admit to wanting to know the reason for it probably as much as he wants to tell me, which is much more than I should.

We told Amy and Jack that we'd take over the clean-up duties so that they could take the rest of the night off. They've done so much for this wedding that it only seems right, and it gives Nate and me a nice neutral ground on which to talk things over. Neutral ground is good; with Nate it's the least dangerous. Nate's standing on one side of the long picnic table, and I'm on the other. We're both holding huge black plastic bags: one for trash, the other for recycling.

Nate dumps paper plates with uneaten bits of food on them into his bag, and I toss remnants of wine into the grass before throwing the plastic cups into the bag to be recycled. The crickets are chirping, and there's a soft breeze in the air. It's light enough to cool our skin, but not strong enough to make a mess of what's left on the picnic table.

The two of us are quiet, a silence that's not altogether comfortable. I think he's waiting for me to ask him why his sister thinks that he missed his flight from Dallas when he'd told me that it was delayed until the next morning. He seems kind of uneasy about it, and because I always think the worst, I assume that it's because he had me pegged as an easy target for airport sex and he isn't quite ready to own up to that yet. I mean, I *was* an easy target for airport sex; I was looking for it, for crying out loud. But knowing that would ruin the whimsy of the flirting, the magnetism that I felt when we were together. I want him to tell me the truth, but at the same time I don't want to know it at all.

"Nate," I begin. His eyes snap up to meet mine like he's been waiting for just that one signal to confess. So, he does.

"I lied to you that night," he says, his eyes searching mine. "My flight *was* canceled because of the storm, but I booked one for later that evening. I was just killing time in the bar; I wanted to catch the end of a game. And then you walked in." He takes a deep breath and sighs, and there isn't anything in the world that could make me look away. "I was glued to the seat, Callie. I couldn't get up, I couldn't leave. I *had* to keep talking to you, I can't explain it. It was… as necessary to me as breathing."

"Then why did you lie?" My voice cracks as the words come out.

"Strangely enough, because I didn't want you to think I was using you. I can see now that wasn't the best plan. My mom, she tracks my flights, and I didn't want to have to explain why-"

"Why you skipped your flight to have sex with some woman you met in a bar?" I try to sound lighthearted about it all, but it falls flat.

"No," he says, closing the distance between us. Without even realizing it, I've walked a few steps towards him. Nate drops the bag, then reaches out for my hand. He holds just my fingers, lightly skimming the pad of his thumb across my nails. "I didn't ask you to leave the bar to have sex with you. I mean, I wanted to have sex with you. I *want* to have sex with you." He lets out a breathy laugh as he shakes his head, and the frustrated smile makes a warmth blossom in my chest. It's cute, the way he stumbles over the words, and he looks at our entwined fingers as he continues. "If you had just wanted to talk that night? I would've sat there and talked to until the sun came up. I would've missed ten flights if I had to."

He squeezes my hand, looking down at me, and the soft light from the lanterns makes his perfect face seem almost ethereal. My breath catches, right in my throat. I want to ask him why, why he wanted to talk to me so badly. Me, the girl whose father left and whose boyfriend turned to another woman for comfort. The girl who's never been quite good enough to make people want to stick around. But somehow, he wanted to.

He searches my eyes, and maybe he knows. Maybe he can see all the doubt inside of me.

"You flipped a switch in me that had been off for a long time," he says. "That night, with you, everything just…lit up."

My heart skips, and the air around me feels so heavy all of a sudden. I don't care about cleaning up or about the trash we're going to leave out here, I don't care about anything other than Nate's smile, and the warmth of his hand, the way his skin feels against mine. I want to feel his hands on me, everywhere.

I slide my fingers through his and we just go together, like my palm was made to fit against his. I lead him across the yard and into the house, through the living room and down the long hallway that leads to our rooms. We pass mine, and walk into his. I turn on the light and close the door.

Nate looks a little surprised, and I want to kiss that surprise right out of him. He has questions, I know he does. I don't have many answers, not yet. Maybe I never will, but I think he understands that about me. He understands a lot about me without really knowing all that much. He's brought back some of the confidence I lost when I found Ethan cheating on me all those months ago. He's made me feel desirable again; it's something I've been missing for far too long.

I untangle our fingers and bring both of my hands to rest on his chest, using his body as leverage as I push myself up on my tiptoes to press my mouth against his. The kiss is soft and tender; very slow, and exactly what I need. Nate's hands come to rest on my hips, steadying me, his fingertips slipping beneath my shirt, branding the skin there. I pull away for just a second to unzip his sweatshirt.

"Callie," Nate says, his voice very tight. "What…" My fingertips stretch across the taut muscles on his abdomen, up along his chest, and the question gets caught in his throat.

As I slide the sweatshirt off his shoulders and into a puddle on the floor, I whisper, "You flipped a switch."

Chapter FOURTEEN

*N*ate cradles my face in his hands, his eyes locked with mine as he gently drags the pads of his thumbs along my overheated cheeks. There are specks of gold buried under all that blue. I've never noticed them before, even though I've been close enough to see them. Maybe I never truly looked for them; maybe I've been too afraid to really see them, been too afraid to look deep enough to see the emotion that hides beneath the surface of Nate's beautiful, expressive eyes.

The air between us holds a current; it's charged with something that's making every single nerve in my body stand on end. Every time Nate touches me, the electricity doubles, creating this sublime, almost unbearable surge of energy around us. It's so completely unlike our last time together, but still incredibly familiar. Everything about this feels amazing, wonderful.

It feels inevitable.

Nate's hands slide back and cradle my head as he gives me a gentle, tender kiss. Then those soft, perfect lips ghost across my cheek and brush against the shell of my ear. He buries his face in my hair, breathing deep, and I cling to him, running my fingers through the short hair at the nape of his neck, tugging gently the way I know he likes. One of his arms bands around my back, the other around my waist, and he holds me so tight. Tight enough that I think he's trying to imprint my body with his, tight enough that I think he might be afraid to let me go. Like if he lets me go, I'll disappear.

I want to tell him that I'm here, *I'm here*, I'm not going anywhere, but I can't tell him that. Trying to convince him otherwise would ruin this anyway.

He lifts my shirt over my head, tossing it to the side and then he unclasps my bra, sliding it down my shoulders. His fingertips gently ghost across my collarbone, down the valley between my breasts. His palms slide up and down my sides, cupping the swell of my breasts before the pads of his thumbs tease my nipples. He touches me very slowly, testing out all the ways he can make my body respond to him, and he watches me like he's trying to commit every single second of this to memory. Then his mouth and tongue follow the path his hands have just taken.

I let my hands explore his chest. I memorize the ridge of every muscle, the raised plane of every scar. I taste the salty sweetness of his skin, licking and sucking and nipping him with my teeth, doubling my efforts whenever he gasps or sighs or groans, which is often.

Curling my fingers around the waistband of his jeans, I pull him with me as I walk backwards, falling onto the bed when the backs of my knees hit the mattress. Nate laughs, god it's my favorite sound, and I make quick work of his zipper, pulling his jeans and boxers down until they fall around his ankles. I skim my fingernails along Nate's upper thigh, across the dips in his hips, drawing a light hiss from his mouth and making goosebumps bloom all over his tanned skin. I slide my palm down his erection and his head tilts back as he exhales in complete satisfaction. I can't help but smile, and I'm driven by this newfound power that I feel just knowing that I have this gorgeous man completely at my mercy.

My hands slide from his hips to the curve of his ass, and I spread my legs as I grip him, giving him room to come closer. I lick him from shaft to tip, gently taking him into my mouth. I hollow out my cheeks, taking him as far into my mouth as I can, and every muscle in Nate's body seems to tense up, although he still seems very relaxed. His hands tangle almost lazily through my hair as he watches me sucking him, his eyes a little unfocused and his lids hooded to the point where I can only make out the faintest hint of blue. Just when he's on the brink of coming—I can tell by the way his breathing speeds up and the way my name is falling from his lips, like he's praying and begging at the same time—he gently pushes me back on the bed, sliding me up towards the headboard. He holds himself up over me as he reaches over and grabs a condom out of his nightstand, then he finds a pillow somewhere behind me, fluffing it up before he lifts my head and slides the pillow underneath it.

Nate smiles down at me, one hand gripping the sheets beside my head, the other one possessively splayed across the side of my neck. I reach up and brush my fingers along the corner of his mouth, luxuriating in the feeling of his stubble beneath my fingers. He turns his head, kissing my palm, then he kisses a trail down my wrist, my inner arm, across my breasts, down my stomach. He kneels between my legs and clasps his hand around my ankle, bringing it up to rest on his shoulder. He kisses the inside of my calf and I laugh, which makes him smile against my skin. He kisses his way down to my knee, where he nips a bit of skin between his teeth, then continues down the inside of my thigh, brushing his whiskers along the spots that he knows will make me squirm. I reach up and thread our fingers together, my right hand, his left, and he squeezes my fingers before letting them go.

"Nate," I whisper, so desperate to feel him in the one place he's so purposefully ignored. I expect him to tell me to be patient, but he doesn't. He spreads me open and licks my clit, slowly at first, but he speeds up to match the quickness of my breath. He pushes his fingers inside of me, curling them up when I arch my back. We are an endless circuit of action and reaction; he intently watches me, adjusting his plan on the fly. He doubles-down on the moves that bring me closer to the edge and does away with the ones that don't. I'm so close, *so close,* but when his blue eyes meet mine as he lovingly strokes my hip with his free hand, a pang of affection strikes me deep in my chest, swelling up and wrapping itself around my heart.

I realize that over the last year or so I've allowed myself to become accustomed to fucking; I've settled for the simple rush of release, of following a checklist. Do this to get that, get that to feel this. I haven't been so intimately connected to someone in so long, the feeling is overwhelming. I reach down and run my fingers through Nate's hair, pressing my head back against the pillow as my orgasm slowly washes over me, warm and wonderful. He slowly rubs his hands up and down my thighs, pressing kisses there as my breathing slows and my heartbeat stops thundering in my ears.

I sit up and unwrap the condom, unrolling it down the length of Nate's erection. He's looking at me strangely, like maybe something's wrong, and absolutely nothing is wrong, but everything is different. I don't think I have the words to explain it, no matter how much I wish that I did.

"C'mere," I tell him, crooking my finger.

He leans down, hands planted firmly on either side of my hips. I gently take his face in my hands, letting the tip of my nose skim across his cheekbones, his chin. And then our lips barely touch and we breathe each other in until I move forward little and he does too, our mouths connecting in a kiss that's long and deep. I pull him down on top of me, letting him settle between my legs.

He looks down at me, eyes swimming with so many emotions. "Callie-"

"Put your arm around me," I whisper, just wanting him to do what I say without asking me any questions. "Around my back."

He slides his hand just below my shoulder blades until I can feel is fingers pressing into my side, then he pushes a strand of hair off my face with his free hand. "Are you okay?"

I nod, trying not to cry. I'm okay. I'm more okay than I've ever been, actually, but I just *need* this, my way.

I push my hips up, taking Nate by surprise as he slips inside me, and I wrap my legs around his waist, drawing him deeper. My arms wind around his shoulders, and he lets out a small, shaky breath as his eyes meet mine.

"Like this, okay?" I say, clinging to him. He barely has any room, but he'll make it work. "Just like this."

He nods, not really able to say anything, or maybe there just isn't anything to say. He presses his forehead to mine as he moves, and my breath catches in my throat as I start to ask him to kiss me. But he knows, he always knows what I need, so his lips meet mine as we rock together, and I hold him like I'm never going to let go. Like I wouldn't let him go, like I can't. And I love the way his skin feels against mine, the way his kisses are a little unfocused because I'm making him feel so good that he can't catch his breath. I love the way he makes my whole body lock up right before I come, but he keeps going, keeps pushing me until I've taken every ounce of pleasure from him that I can and my bones are like jelly. He follows soon after, and when we're both completely sapped of energy and lying in a breathless mess of limbs and bodies, Nate rolls over onto his back, pulling me on top of him. I lie draped across his chest, my head coming to rest in the crook of his neck. I pull myself onto him until every single inch of our skin that can touch is touching.

I want to melt into him, want to fill all the empty spaces inside of him. He kisses my forehead as I draw tiny hearts across his chest with my fingertip. His breathing slows and evens out, but he wraps his arms around me, snuggling me against him, wanting me closer even in his sleep.

I close my eyes and smile. Unlike our first night together in Dallas, this time there isn't a single part of me that wants to run. Worse than that, I want to stay.

Wanting to stay is the scariest feeling of all.

Once again, daylight seems to come much too quickly when I'm lying in Nate's arms, but this time I'm not running from it. I'm snuggled against his chest, my head resting in the crook of his neck. His fingers run through my hair, gently pulling in a way that would put me back to sleep if I wasn't so desperate to remember every second of this morning. Our legs are tangled together beneath the sheets, and everything about it feels so natural that I can't imagine there was a time when I ever felt comfortable anywhere else. But I only let myself dwell on that thought for a second, because it tends to lead me down roads that make me think too much.

"What's your favorite breakfast food?" Nate asks, twirling the ends of my hair around his finger.

"It's a tie," I tell him, enjoying the beat of his heart beneath my hand, where it's splayed across his chest.

"Between what?"

"Between my desire for delicious food and my desire to live past forty."

"So what are they?" He presses a kiss against my forehead, his stubble deliciously rough against my skin.

"Well, first there's bacon, I mean…obviously."

"Mmmm, bacon."

I like the way Nate's voice sounds with my ear pressed against his chest.

"Bacon for breakfast, bacon for lunch, bacon for dinner. Bacon for snack time," I say. "Bacon, bacon, bacon."

"So what's the other favorite?" he asks, quietly laughing.

"Raisin Bran. I love it, I can't help myself," I say, reaching over to twine my fingers with his. Everything about him is so warm, it's impossible for me to not touch him, not want to be near to him. "It's good for a healthy heart."

"Fiber is important," he agrees, bringing my fingers up to his lips. He presses a kiss there, and I look up at him just in time to catch his smile.

"Regularity and all that. Plus, raisins are pretty awesome."

Nate laughs. "I can tell this conversation is taking a Wright family turn," he says, and I think back to the conversations I've witnessed with his family that inevitably go somewhere gross.

"Ask me something else then."

"Is anything off limits?"

I can feel the change in his breathing, the rise and fall of his chest. Maybe that should be a warning to me to say that yes, there are some things off limits, but I feel like an open book to him. I don't know why exactly, but I don't feel compelled to hide anything right now.

"Nope, nothing," I reply.

He hesitates for a few seconds, and I feel my pulse quicken.

"Tell me about your family," he says quietly. "You know all about mine, but I don't know anything about yours."

"To be fair, I just kind of stumbled into your family," I reply, trying to buy myself some time.

"My mom told me that she wants to take you with her on a trip to New York. That's a little more than a stumble."

"I think she felt bad because I was standing there when she asked Gabby to go." I hope he can't hear the undercurrent of disappointment in my voice.

"Nah," he says, skimming his fingertips along my spine. The simple action makes all of my nerves stand on end, makes it difficult for me to concentrate. "She's not swayed by guilt. If she asked you to go, it's because she wants you there. And you're avoiding my question." He plants another kiss on the top of my head. "You don't have to answer it if you don't want to."

Strangely enough, the fact that he gives me an out makes me want to give him an answer. "What do you want to know?" I ask, looking up and meeting his gaze.

"Everything."

That *would* be his answer. "My mother was born Ella Mae Sampson in Plano, Texas during a heatwave in the summer of nineteen sixty-five."

Nate laughs. "Smartass."

I take a minute to gather my thoughts before I start talking again. "My mom, she's short like I am, and we look kind of alike. She's got this pretty blonde hair that's kind of wavy, and she always wears it pulled back, away from her face. She's crazy smart, and she worked really hard to put herself through college after my dad left us. She's a vice president at a marketing firm. Actually, she was going to come this weekend, but she had to go on a trip for work at the last minute." Even though I've only been gone for a few days, talking about my mother makes me miss her so much that it hurts.

"She sounds amazing."

"She is. She's one of the most dynamic people I've ever met. I honestly don't know what my life would be like if I didn't have her."

"Your dad, he left?"

I nod. "He did. He hung around a while after the divorce. He came to see me every other weekend for about a year. Then one day I waited for him to pick me up, but he never came. I haven't seen him since."

I can feel the hitch in Nate's breathing, and his arms tighten around me. "How old were you when this happened?"

"Eleven. It was difficult for me to accept at the time," I admit. I've never told anyone this, not even Ethan. "I didn't want to believe that he could just pick up and leave me like that. So I used to pretend that he realized he made a mistake and came back, and that he would watch me from afar. Like, I pretended that he was in the crowds at the mall, in the throng of parents that sat in the bleachers during my softball games. It was really pathetic."

"It's not pathetic," Nate says, his voice kind of broken. "But I'll never understand how anyone could abandon their child like that."

"I think it's easy for some people." I trace a tiny heart on his chest with my fingertip to distract myself.

"How could it be?"

"I don't know," I tell him. "But the scary thing is that sometimes you don't know who those people are until it's too late."

"Callie," he whispers, so quietly that I almost can't hear it.

"He tried to get in touch with me a couple of years ago," I admit. This is yet another thing that I haven't told anyone, not even my own mother.

"What'd you do?"

"I didn't do anything." There's an unexpected wave of shame that hits me when I admit it; it comes from nowhere, nearly taking my breath away. "I just never called him back."

"Not even to tell him how much he hurt you?"

I let out a small laugh. "Why would I want him to know that?"

Nate shifts onto his side and slides his hand down until his arm is wrapped around my waist. Even though our bodies aren't in contact the way they were before, this position seems much more intimate. I can't hide from him here; his eyes are searching mine.

"I think it's good to let people know when they've hurt you," he says, and there isn't a hint of judgment in his tone. "How else do they learn?"

"Why is it my responsibility to get him to be a better person?" I try not to sound as hateful as I feel.

"It's not," he replies, a sad smile on his lips. "Maybe I have an idealized view of the world, I don't know."

He reaches over and cups my cheek, and I close my eyes as I lean into him. He definitely has an idealized view of the world, but I like that about him, especially since I'm cynical enough for the both of us.

"Nah," I reply, attempting to tease him. "Not you."

"Your feelings matter, Callie. You know, I've been an asshole in my life... more times than I care to admit. And yeah, I knew then that I was behaving like an asshole, but when I finally found out how it really affected those people—when they told me how badly I'd hurt them—it changed me. And, you know, the ones that I hurt, some of them don't get the benefit of seeing me become a better person. But it was those people who taught me how to treat the people I love." He swallows hard when he's finished speaking, and I can tell that he's admitted to more than he meant to.

I'm not sure if he said what he said because he wants me to know that he's made mistakes and he's learned from them, or because he thinks somehow I can help my father become a better man. Maybe he thinks it'll help me to vent, or maybe he just said it to say it. But there's something about the sentiment that touches this disillusioned place inside of me, that makes me feel the faintest glimmer of hope, however fleeting it may be.

Right now, the only thing I want in this world is to kiss him. So that's exactly what I do.

Chapter
FIFTEEN

"What is this?" Nate asks, lifting my purse into his lap, examining it like it's some kind of science experiment. He's perched on the edge of my bed, waiting impatiently for me to finish getting ready so that we can head down to the rehearsal dinner. I keep telling him to go ahead without me, but he refuses. Even though he's being kind of a pain in my ass right now, I can't deny that I like having him nearby.

"That's my purse," I say, laughing at the confusion on his face.

"It's bigger than you are, Callie."

It's a black leather hobo bag which is a little too big, yes, and admittedly it does have a lot of…well, crap in it.

"It is not," I tell him.

He opens the clasp and peers inside. "Hello…hello…hello," he says, each word getting quieter as he imitates an echo.

"You can be a smartass or you can be nosy. You can't be both at the same time." I dab some perfume behind my ears and on my wrists before I lean over the dresser to get a good look in the mirror so I can apply my lip gloss.

"How do you find anything in here?"

I shrug. "Sometimes I can't. I've been known to throw things in there and find them months later. I'm a bit of a slob," I say as I spread a glossy pink across my lips. "It's one of my flaws."

Nate nods as he snaps the bag shut, seemingly filing that information away for later. Then he leans back on the bed, his hands splayed out on either side of him, holding him up.

"You should go down, I'm going to be a few more minutes."

He's sitting behind me; I can only see him through the reflection in the mirror, but I watch the sly grin that spreads across his lips, and I recognize that look in his eyes. It's almost predatory; it sends a shiver up my spine. He leans forward, resting his elbows on his knees.

"Why would I leave when I've got an excellent view right where I am?" I feel Nate's fingertips trailing up the back of my leg, underneath the hem of my skirt. It's a tingling, light feeling that spreads throughout my body. I can't really put a name to it, but I feel it every time he touches me, every time he looks at me, and I know he hears my breath catch. When he does, he presses his hands to the sides of my legs, turning me until I'm facing him. He stands, sliding his hands up, up, up until they grip my waist, and he lifts me up onto the dresser.

"Nate," I whisper, just to hear his name.

He starts at my neck, peppering kisses across my skin before he drags his lips down along the neckline of my dress where he plants his lips again and again. His hands are still gripping my waist and he pulls me forward to the end of the dresser, until he's settled between my legs. His stubble is rough against my skin, and I know it'll leave red splotches everywhere, but I don't care, *I don't care* as long as he keeps his mouth and his hands on my body. He doesn't remove my dress, doesn't so much as slip his hand beneath the fabric. He just ghosts his hand down the valley between my breasts, and it's like every single inch of me is on fire.

Then he kneels down, bringing my right leg to rest against the dresser and my left to rest over his shoulder. He drags his teeth along the sensitive skin on the inside of my thigh, nipping and kissing his way further up.

"We're going to be late," I whisper, and when he opens his eyes, they're dark and intense, clouded by challenge. I skim my nails along the sides of his head and down the line of his jaw, scratching the stubble there. It's prickly against my fingers, and Nate sighs as my hands fall away.

"We'll be late then," he says, his voice all gravely and low.

"But it's your brother's rehearsal dinner."

He laughs and shakes his head. "Callie, do *not* talk about my brother right now."

I run my fingers through his hair again, and when he closes his eyes and takes a deep breath, I can tell I've made up for my mistake.

"Still," I whisper, cupping his cheek. "Late."

"I bet I don't even need five minutes." Nate gives me this cocky little grin, and I decide to challenge him, even though I know he's probably right.

"That's not something to brag about."

"I beg to differ," he says, sliding his finger along the edge of my panties, making me squirm. "In this situation, it says nothing about my stamina and everything about how much I turn you on."

I know it won't take five minutes, but I like the determination in his eyes as he bunches my skirt up around my waist. He pushes my panties to the side and I feel his breath on me, right before he takes one long, decisive lick. I let out a sigh and rest my head against the mirror, running my hand through his hair as my breathing speeds up.

"*Oh*. Nate," I whisper, and I can feel his smile as his mouth moves against me, sucking and dragging and licking. His other hand creeps up my thigh, and I lace my fingers with his, just wanting to be connected to him in some other way. The pad of his thumb moves in slow circles along the back of my hand, mimicking the torturous movement of his tongue. I grip his hand tighter as I feel that rising tide of pleasure welling up inside of me, and I press on the back of his head so that his mouth is just where I want it, where I *need* it to be. Just when I'm ready to fall apart, there's a knock on my door.

"Callie," Shelby says, practically yelling. "Dinner's starting, are you going to come?"

"Yes," I breathe, not talking to her at all. Because yes…*yes*.

Nate laughs with a gentle hum that nearly undoes me.

"Callie?"

"I'll be there in a few," I yell, hoping she doesn't catch the wavering in my voice.

"You're going to be late."

"I said I'm coming!" I yell, and I could laugh at the absurdity of it all, because I *am* coming, I am, I am, and I feel the sparks from it all throughout my body. My breaths are ragged, and Nate's mouth is still on me, pushing me along as I ride out this wave. Our fingers are still entwined, my hand rubbing lazy circles on the back of his head. It's not long before he presses tender kisses along the inside of my thighs, and he reaches up and lowers my dress.

I want to kiss that smug smile off his face, so I pull him close and I smile too as our lips meet slowly and softly. He's still grinning when he pulls away, and I swipe the pad of my thumb along his bottom lip to wipe off the pink gloss that's smeared there.

"What's with the face?" I ask.

He shrugs as he leans in close, planting his hands on either side of my hips. I nuzzle against his neck and breathe deep as his lips brush the shell of my ear.

"Two minutes and sixteen seconds," he whispers.

*A*fter dinner we're all gathered around the patio, spread out in different groups, talking and laughing. I find myself orbiting Nate without really meaning to; I just feel this intense desire to be close to him, and for once I'm not over thinking it.

"So, no to the cliff diving," he says, laughing through a smile as he brings his beer bottle to his lips. "I kind of figured you'd say that after your tire swing-slash-eel experience. You either love the feeling of falling or you hate it."

I lean against the short brick wall that lines the patio, splaying my hands out on either side of me as Nate steps forward, blocking my view of the crowd. It's like he wants me all to himself, and tonight, I'm all too happy to let him have me.

"It's not the falling that I have the issue with," I tell him, tilting my head back until our eyes meet. "I love that hollow, tingling feeling as my stomach drops. At that point you've already given up the control, and you can enjoy it. It's the standing on the edge of the solid, safe earth and deciding to jump that drives me crazy."

Nate looks at me for a long while, a sad smile pulling at his lips. His hand cups my cheek and I snuggle against it before he runs his fingers through my hair, cradling the back of my neck as he touches his forehead with mine.

"Not everything needs to be planned out, Callie. Fly by the seat of your pants for once," he says softly, and I know he's not talking about cliff diving. Maybe we never were. Our lips connect for just a few seconds, and even though it's a sweet kiss—innocent, even—it puts every nerve in my body on overdrive.

I turn to my right and see Gabby. She's standing with Ben, Marco and Emily, but her eyes are on Nate and me. When she excuses herself from their conversation, I touch Nate's forearm and nod in her direction to let him know that I'm going to talk to her. We meet in the middle of the room, and she quickly takes my hand and leads me over to the corner, near the hammock. She gives me a knowing smirk, and my stomach sinks because I know what I'm in for.

"He's got it so bad," she says in a singsongy way, like we're on the playground back in grade school. "And he's not the only one."

I glare at her, partly because she interrupted us and partly because she's right. "You promised no matchmaking, Gabby."

"I didn't!"

"You did too, you promised that morning in the truck," I remind her.

She smiles, and there's something gentle about it that makes me relax. "I meant that I didn't do any matchmaking. This is…it's all you two. Everyone can see it."

"See what?" I ask, playing innocent.

"The way he looks at you, Callie. The way you look at him. If you think this is just some fling-"

"It is a fling," I say, interrupting her. "And I'm enjoying it while it lasts. Don't ruin the two days I have left by trying to make this into more than it is."

"Callie," she sighs. "Don't be stupid. What do you think is going to happen when this is over?"

"What I *know* will happen is that you and Ben will go on your honeymoon. I'll go back to Dallas and Nate will go back to Boulder, and I'll look back on this fondly."

"QUIET EVERYBODY!!!" Madeline yells. Nate's holding her, and she seems embarrassed by the sudden attention as the room quiets, so she tucks her head into his neck to shield her face. He walks up the few steps that lead into the guest house so that everyone can see him, and his eyes are drawn to mine in the crowd. He winks at me, and I know he's doing whatever he's about to do in order to break up this conversation because he can see how uncomfortable I am. I could (and would) kiss him for it if it wouldn't send Gabby into a frenzy.

Nate clears his throat. "Mad here has something she'd like to say to her Uncle Ben and new Aunt Gabby," he says with a smile, gently nudging Madeline with his chin.

Gabby, never one to abandon an unfinished conversation turns to me before motioning in Nate's direction, like she wants to remind me of what I have right there in front of me. "You're really going to make yourself miserable to prove a point?"

"I'm not trying to prove anything," I tell her, and it's the truth. She thinks I'm going to be miserable if I don't give myself a shot to be with Nate, but misery I can deal with. It's the inevitable broken heart that kills.

*I*t's getting late, and all the guests are beginning to say their goodnights and go back to their rooms to prepare for the big day ahead of us tomorrow. At the same time tomorrow I'll be standing here with all the same people, wearing a beautiful dress, and Gabby will have tied herself to Ben for the rest of her life. The remarkable thing—to me, at least—is that she isn't even the slightest bit nervous about it. Sure, she's worried about the ceremony, but the commitment part of the equation doesn't even make her break a sweat.

I'm self-aware enough to admit that I'm jealous of her in that regard. Not that I *want* to get married, but I always wanted it to be an option. Now it seems as unattainable to me as winning a lottery jackpot. I think back to what Nate told me earlier this morning about telling the people who have hurt me what they've done. Maybe there's some benefit to doing that beyond helping those people to not make the same mistakes again. Maybe the closure would help me move on. To what, exactly, I don't know…but maybe that's not important right now.

Across the yard, Ethan's sitting on a bench by himself. His elbows are resting on his knees, and he's got the neck of a beer bottle clasped between his thumb and index finger, gently swinging it back and forth. It occurs to me that while I'm not ready to talk to my father about how I felt when he left my mother and me, I am ready to talk to Ethan about our breakup. Maybe it will help him as much as it would help me, and as much as I shouldn't want to help him, I do. Once upon a time he was my friend, and sometimes I do miss that, even if the sting of betrayal does taint those memories.

I step off the porch and walk across the lawn, and if Ethan's surprised when I sit next to him, he doesn't show it. His gaze is fixed somewhere off to our right, and when I turn my head I see that he's looking at Emily. Madeline's sleeping, draped across Emily's lap. Emily runs her fingers through Madeline's hair as she talks to Jessa. I'm not quite sure where this fierce protective surge comes from, given the fact that I barely know Emily, but it's there and I can't ignore it.

"Don't screw around on her, Ethan. She doesn't deserve that," I say. I'm surprised at my bluntness, but Ethan doesn't seem to be offended by it.

Ethan's quiet for a minute, watching his girlfriend, hopefully letting what I just said sink in. "You two are friends now?" He finally replies.

"We don't have to be friends for me to know that I don't want that to happen to her."

Looking at me with sad eyes, Ethan's mouth opens and shuts, like he wants to say something but doesn't quite know how to put it. I decide to speak for him instead, because I need to get this out while I'm ready to say it.

"I'm just going to say this, okay? It'll be completely devoid of all the anger and resentment that I've felt for you over the past six months, and after I get it out, you can stop looking at me like a kicked puppy, and I'll stop looking at you like I want to rip your heart out, and maybe things won't be weird for Gabby and Ben anymore," I say in one long breath. "I've been angry with you all this time not because of the cheating, which, yes…it did hurt, but…you took something from me that day, Ethan. You killed my belief in people and my ability to trust them and to take what they say and do at face value. You made me scared to take a chance again." His eyes are locked with mine, and somehow I know that he's listening, that he's taking this to heart. "I had issues with some of those things before I met you, I mean, I'm not going to lay all of this at your feet, but you didn't help any of that. I'm not sure if I'll ever be like I was before. Maybe I'll move past all this and be a stronger, better person. That's what I hope for. And for you, I hope…" I take a deep breath, because it's harder than I expected to say these words. "I hope you have a good life, Ethan. I really do."

Ethan blinks his watery eyes, and I can practically hear him swallow. "I'm sorry that I hurt you, Callie."

"I know," I say, reaching out and squeezing his forearm. "I forgive you."

His eyes shift back to Emily, uncertainty written on his face.

"Let her go if it gets to be too much." He nods but doesn't look at me, and I take that as my cue to leave. I've only taken a few steps before he speaks.

"Nate's a good guy."

I could laugh, because Ethan is the very last person I'd ever want vouching for any potential love interests, and I want to tell him that I don't need him of all people to point out Nate's goodness. But I don't want to end this conversation with bitchiness; it would undermine everything I was trying to do here.

Instead, I tell him the truth.

"I know."

 hen I return to the patio, Nate's leaning on the railing, off to the side and away from the crowd. I can tell just by the expression on his face that he saw me talking to Ethan, and when he looks up, his eyes are full of questions. Instinctively I know that he won't ask me what we talked about, because he knows that it really isn't any of his business. The strange thing is I want it to be his business. For whatever reason, I don't want him to worry about it, or to let any thoughts of a reconciliation between Ethan and me even enter his mind.

Nate stands when I get closer. His arm slips around my waist, fingers curled along the side of my hip, and it's comforting here in this spot where our bodies seem to fit together perfectly. He leans down, brushing his lips against my ear. "Is everything okay?"

I take a deep breath as I nod, then my eyes meet his. "I was just trying to help Ethan become a better person."

Nate's eyebrows knit together in confusion before a slow, understanding smile spreads across his face, brightening his eyes.

"Do you want to get out of here?" I ask.

"Yes," he says softly, resting his hand on the small of my back as he leads me over to where Gabby and Ben are standing so that we can say goodnight. I hug the two of them and tell Gabby I'll see her first thing in the morning, ignoring the smug look on her face when Nate twines his fingers with mine as we turn and make our way across the yard.

He rubs slow circles on the back of my hand as I follow him into his room, where he turns on the lights and gently shuts the door behind us. He presses a soft, lingering kiss to my lips as I reach up and loosen his tie, slipping it from around his neck and letting it fall into a puddle on the floor. We both work on undoing the buttons on his shirt and once that's off, I fumble with the zipper on his pants. Once's he's finally naked, he makes quick work of my dress, sliding it off of my shoulders until it falls at my feet. Nate unclasps my bra and I pull down my panties, and then he skims one hand across my breast and down to my hip as he walks me backwards to the bed.

Nate sits in the center of the mattress and I make myself comfortable between his crossed legs, wrapping my legs around his waist and my arms around his neck. Each beat of my frenzied heart pushes me closer to him, and every last nerve in my body is pulsing with want for him. He must feel the same about me if the hardness against my thigh is any indication, but we take our time and just kiss each other. Just hold each other. Just be.

We spend most of the night wrapped around each other. Sometimes we doze, sometimes we touch. Sometimes my back is pressed against Nate's chest and his lips are warm on my neck and he presses his palm against my thigh, opening me up to him, and I sigh as he slips inside of me like it's where he's always belonged. There's nothing frenzied about it; it's slow and purposeful, like neither one of us are chasing any kind of pleasure other than the kind that comes from just being together. We spend all night learning each other's bodies, both by taste and by touch.

Very early in the morning, when we're both quiet and still, I don't waste time thinking about the inevitable destruction of my already broken heart. I'm just happy to hold Nate and be held by him, for however long it lasts.

Chapter
SIXTEEN

Gabby stares out of the French doors in the Wrights' living room, watching the crowd of friends and family taking their seats in the backyard. She's so beautiful with her perfectly styled hair and lovely dress that it's actually difficult for me to look at her. She's as radiant as the sun; as blindingly bright and warm. I walk over to her, holding her bouquet in my right hand and mine in my left.

"Last chance for us to make a clean getaway," I say, shifting the flowers in my hands so that I can smooth out her veil. "I'll knock out Jasmine and Shelby, and we'll get at least a fifteen minute head start."

"You *wish* you could knock me out, Kirkpatrick," Jasmine teases, the hint of a challenge behind her eyes.

"All I want is to be down at that altar." Gabby looks at me with a gleam in her eyes, and I can see how sure she is about what it is that she's about to do. "I want to be his wife."

I want to be that sure about something for the rest of my life.

There's a floor length mirror to the side of the door, and I take a look at my reflection. I look as pretty as I feel in this pale pink chiffon dress with my hair falling across my shoulders in sculpted curls because it just didn't want to behave for the hairdresser this morning. The dress falls to just below my knees, and I like the way the shimmering strappy heels I'm wearing make my legs look.

"Are you about done primping for your boyfriend out there?" Shelby asks, arching her brow as she shoots me a disapproving glance. "Gab's getting married in five minutes, and you've seen her with Ben. This one's gonna stick, so you won't get another chance to see her in a wedding dress."

I stick my tongue out at her and she smiles. I try not to be too obvious about the way I stand on my tiptoes and look out the window to find Nate. My stomach does a cute little flip when I see him, looking so handsome in his light gray suit.

"Are you ladies ready? It's time," Amy's friend Diane says as she pulls open the doors.

The murmur of the crowd quiets as a trio of violins start playing. Shelby squares her shoulders and steps out onto the patio. Jasmine takes her place in the doorway, ready to go next. I hand Gabby her bouquet, and she wraps her fingers around mine, giving them a gentle squeeze. There are tears brimming in her eyes—the happiest kind—as she gives me a knowing smile.

"You look beautiful," I tell her, swallowing past the lump in my throat. "You're going to be so happy, Gab. You deserve all the happiness in the world."

"So do you," she whispers. "I love you, Callie."

I nod, smiling. "I love you too. Good luck, sweetie."

Gabby lets go of my hand just as Diane touches my shoulder, letting me know that it's my turn to go. I step out onto the green, *green* grass of the pristine lawn, and I look everywhere but at Nate, because I'm afraid that I'll walk too fast if I see his face. Instead I focus on putting one foot in front of the other and walking down the aisle between the rows of pristine white chairs that hold all of Ben and Gabby's loved ones. Amy gives me a smile through watery eyes as I walk past her, and I take the three steps up onto the altar.

The music changes to a soft, swelling march as Gabby steps out of the house. I watch her through my own tears as she walks down the aisle, Ben looking so in love that it seems like he's having a difficult time not running across the yard and taking her in his arms. And the cynic in me—bastard that it is—makes itself known. I can't help but think about all the couples who have done this before them, who have walked down aisles and stood on altars where they promised to love each other forever. Couples who—years later—wind up fighting over kitchen tables and antique lamps in the comfort of the offices of their five-hundred-dollar-per-hour divorce lawyers. Did they all start off looking like Gabby and Ben?

I think about Amy and Jack, holding hands in the front row, who somehow managed to beat the odds. Is it predetermined when couples walk down the aisle which ones will make it and which ones won't? Or does everyone start out with the same shot, and the choices they make throughout the years either bring them together or push them apart? My head spins at the thought of it all. Getting married, hell...even giving your heart to someone is like jumping off a cliff. How can people make this kind of commitment not knowing what will happen when they land?

People like my mom and dad just couldn't make it work. But there are also people like Amy and Jack. And people like Gabby and Ben, so in love with each other that it both inspires and scares me.

And then there's Nate. Standing across the aisle from me, his eyes locked with mine, smiling at me like the whole world has fallen away.

When he looks at me like that, I wish it would.

I reach out and take Gabby's bouquet.

"Dearly beloved, we are gathered here today..."

inner starts just as the sun goes down, and the twinkle lights draped from the poles of the canopy combined with the soft candlelight from the tapered arrangements on the tables cast an ethereal glow across the tent. There's a dance floor on the far side of it with a deejay booth in the corner, but he's playing soft music now, mainly drowned out by the buzz of conversation and silverware clinking on china. Dinner is a delicious one: filet with a side of roasted asparagus and mushroom risotto. We're drinking delicious wine, and the company is wonderful. Ben and Gabby just got married, and they're so disgustingly cute. I should be happy—I mean, I *am* happy—but I shouldn't be so caught up in my own thoughts.

I feel like a bundle of nerves and insecurity, and absolutely nothing is helping. Thankfully, I don't think that my distraction is that obvious, or if it is, other people are too wrapped up in the party to notice, which is good. Nate is sitting to my left, cutting steak and asparagus into tiny pieces for Madeline. She's sitting on his lap, giggling. Jessa's sitting a few tables away with her husband, who just arrived this morning. They seem to have fallen on the Wright side of things as far as functional relationships go: they've been married for five years, and they're looking at each other like it's *their* wedding day. Even Ethan and Emily are leaning close to each other, holding hands and sharing smiles.

I seem to be the dysfunctional one in this group. Oddly, it doesn't depress me, it just makes me want to isolate myself so I don't accidentally taint any of these lovely people around me. Especially the one right next to me, who's being so adorably wonderful with his niece that I'm having a difficult time wiping the smile off of my face.

"Are you gonna save a dance for me later?" Nate asks as he spears a piece of meat with his fork.

"Why do I gots ta save it?" Madeline looks up at him with her big, blue, inquisitive eyes.

Nate grins and lets out a small, airy laugh. "It's an expression, Mad. When you want to dance with a pretty girl and you know that lots of other boys are going to ask her too, you want to make sure that she knows you want to be one of those boys. So you ask her to save a dance for you."

Madeline's cute little mouth forms a tiny 'o,' and I can tell that she doesn't quite understand, but she goes along with it anyway. "'Kay."

Nate laughs as Madeline steals the steak from from the end of the fork, popping it in her mouth with a high-pitched hum.

"You're going to save a dance for me later, aren't you?" He gives me a sexy wink that makes my heart ache as much as it makes it flutter.

I nod, not trusting myself to say anything.

Nate's eyebrows scrunch together; he must notice that I've got something on my mind. As soon as he opens his mouth to say something else, Amy stands and clinks her spoon against her wine glass. When the room is quiet, she picks up a microphone and walks over to our table, coming to a stop right in front of Ben and Gabby.

"Thank you all for coming tonight to celebrate my son and my new daughter," Amy says with a smile. I notice that she didn't call Gabby her daughter-in-law, and yet again I feel this surge of affection for this wonderful woman who has welcomed my best friend into her family in every possible way. "My Ben has always been very private. He keeps everything he cares about very closely guarded; he doesn't like to share it with the world. When he was a boy, he was full of big ideas, and he was so smart, but he never wanted to show his father and me anything he was working on before it was finished. He wanted to be sure it was *exactly* the way he wanted it to be before he showed either one of us."

I look over at Ben; his fingers are entwined with Gabby's, and he's looking down at them with a shy smile on his face. Gabby's eye's are trained on Amy.

"When he went off to college in Texas, all he could talk about was the Rangers and the heat and how much he hated his Chem professor. Then one day, he mentioned Gabby. He told Jack how she'd shared her English Lit book with him when he'd forgotten his back at the dorm and didn't have time to go back and get it." Everyone laughs; Ben's forgetfulness is well-known to those who love him. Amy turns and looks at Gabby, then reaches out and takes her hand. "He started talking about her more and more, and finally one day he brought her home to meet us. I knew then, the first time I saw him smile at her, that we'd wind up here someday. My serious boy who loves so deeply and cares so much had finally found a partner who could make him laugh. Gabby is...she's everything I've ever wanted for him. She's exactly the kind of woman I wanted him to marry, and I think his father taught him everything he needs to know about being a loving husband to her." A tear slips down Amy's cheek as she looks over at Jack, and I have to swipe away the tears that are falling down mine.

Nate gently bumps my shoulders with his. He leans in close and whispers, "Wait for it."

"I'm so happy that we're all here to celebrate Ben finding his soulmate, and Gabby marrying her Mr. Wright."

Amy puts the mic down and hugs the two of them as the room erupts in applause.

Even though Nate told me about his mother's love for "Mister Wright with a 'W'-slash-Mister right with an 'R' comparisons," in a teasing way, I thought he'd playfully roll his eyes when she said it. Instead, he looks over at me with an unreadable expression on his face, and the intensity of it is too much for me to bear.

"Are you just going to stare at him all night looking miserable?" Xavier asks as he leads me across the small dance floor.

"I don't look miserable," I tell him, not even bothering to deny the fact that I'm staring at Nate. He's a few couples away, holding Madeline's hands as she balances on the top of his feet, trying to learn a simple box step. I grin watching the two of them, but I know it's a melancholy sort of thing because there's this inexplicable sadness pulling at my heart that I can't quite seem to shake this evening.

"You look miserable, and that's not acceptable." Xavier flashes this sly grin before he dramatically dips me, and I can't help the high-pitched squeal that comes out of my mouth. I laugh as he lifts me up, and lightly smack his shoulder once I'm back on two feet again.

"That's better," he says, pulling me closer. I rest my head in the crook of his neck, glad to be close to someone with no expectations for a little while. We sway together for a minute or two longer, until the song ends. Another one starts up, and soon Xavier is pulling away.

"May I?" Nate asks.

Xavier steps away quickly, knowing my acceptance is a foregone conclusion. I nod, offering Nate a small smile as he takes my hand in his. As usual, the slightest contact with his skin just burns, sets every nerve in my body on end. I take a deep breath as his hand slips around my waist and settles against the small of my back, pulling me closer until my body practically melts into his. I wind my fingers up along his shoulders until my fingertips brush the hair on the nape of his neck. I can feel his heart stuttering against my chest, can feel the way his breath picks up when I touch him like this.

I squeeze my eyes as my stomach twists. I can't imagine allowing myself to keep him.

I can't imagine letting him go.

I wish I could shake this sadness that I've been feeling ever since I stepped onto that altar. I promised myself I wouldn't get involved, and yet here I am, so tangled up in him that I'm having difficulty figuring out how to let go.

If Nate notices my struggle, he doesn't mention it directly. If he sees the indecision behind my eyes, he tries to distract me from it.

"This is a pretty dress," he says, gently sliding his finger below the strap and dragging it over the curve of my shoulder. Goosebumps bloom all over my skin, and I can tell by the look in his eyes that he's pretty pleased with the way he can make my body react to a simple touch. Nate's stubble scratches my cheek as he bends down to whisper in my ear. "It'll look good on my bedroom floor."

I pull away and laugh, rolling my eyes at how cheesy that line is. "You're better than this," I say, teasing him. I close my eyes as he kisses the tip of my nose.

"Fine," he replies, smiling, his finger still gliding across my skin as his blue eyes meet mine. "We'll play a game to see how good I can make you feel while you're still wearing it."

That smile, those words, and his eyes all conspire to make my knees a little weak.

"We have to stay here until Gabby and Ben leave," I tell him, not really sure why I'm discouraging him all of a sudden.

Nate's fingers curl around mine as he brings me closer, pressing our chests together. "We'll make the most of the time we have left."

The way he's misreading my sadness makes my heart ache.

"We're leaving tomorrow." My voice is a little strained. I'm not quite sure why I say it; maybe it's to remind myself of the inevitability of our goodbyes, and maybe it's to remind him.

"What happens then?" Nate's voice is soft, and I'm not even sure that he meant for me to hear the question. I answer it anyway.

"I don't know."

We sway in time with the music, and I turn my head, breathing deep. I wish I could find a way to keep his scent with me forever; I want to bottle it up and carry it around in my purse to remind me of happier times whenever life starts bringing me down. I close my eyes and think of his smile, the one that brings that dimple in his cheek out of hiding and makes his eyes as blue as the sky.

"You could come to Colorado," he says, skimming his fingertips along the exposed skin on my back. "I could come visit you. We could find a way to make it work."

This, *this* is what I didn't want to be thinking about tonight. Or…ever, really, if I'm being honest. I could kick myself, because this is the very thing I was worried about happening when I saw him walk out of the screen door on the porch a few days ago. And I'm such an idiot, because how could I not fall for him? How could anything between us be casual? He's as beautiful inside as he is on the outside, but I just…I can't. I *can't*, and there are no words to explain the fear and the desire that are swirling around in my stomach.

"Callie?" he whispers.

"Can we talk about that later?" I ask, trying so hard to sound like I'm not terrified. I think I've failed, because when I look up at Nate, his eyes are cloudy, his brows furrowed. It's a look that's so out of place on his handsome face that I have to reach up and smooth the crinkle between his eyebrows with the pad of my thumb. Even though his face relaxes, the rest of him is clearly tense.

He doesn't ask about visiting again, but his arms loosen their hold on me, and already he's slipping away.

Better now than later.

*G*abby, Shelby, Jasmine and I stand in Ben's bedroom, helping Gabby finish packing her honeymoon suitcase. I've never been in Ben's room before, but I have to say that it isn't nearly as nice as Nate's. The reason for this is primarily because Ben appears to be a slob.

"This is disgusting," I say, pointing at a pair of boxers that are hanging off of a globe on his desk. I don't even want to know about the chain of events that led to that particular item of clothing being flung there. "Is this what your bedroom looks like in your apartment?"

Gabby throws her hairbrush in her luggage and looks up at me like I've grown a second head. "It's like you don't know me at all," she teases. "I told him to go ahead and be as sloppy as he wanted to be this week, because once that ring is on his finger he won't be throwing his dirty laundry everywhere."

"The ring is already on his finger," I say quietly.

Gabby looks down at her hand and grins. "Yeah, I guess it is."

"I put about a hundred condoms in your bag, so you guys are all set there." Jasmine, the true ambassador for safe sex. "Don't let him knock you up right away. You guys need some time to just chill and be married. And that corporate ladder is harder to climb when you've got an infant hanging off of your arm."

"Infants don't hang," Shelby says, rolling her eyes. "Do you even know anything about babies?"

"No," Jasmine replies. She looks positively disgusted. "And I plan to keep it that way."

"Pay attention to that sage advice," I say, pointing at Jas as I walk over and sit on the top of the suitcase, trying to help condense its contents to the point where one of us will hopefully be able to zip the damn thing.

"Take lots of pictures of the Seine," Jasmine says. "An obscene amount of pictures."

Shelby sighs. "They're going to have better things to do than provide artwork for your ten thousandth living room renovation."

"Yeah," I say, finally able to move the zipper along the top side of the bag. "Like buying me a vintage Chanel clutch. Cream or black, please."

Gabby's standing in front of the mirror that hangs over Ben's dresser, wrapping a pretty silk scarf around her neck. She leans forward, running her finger along the bottom of her lip to clean off any stray lipstick, then puckers her lips. It takes her a few seconds to turn to us, and when she does she's smiling. The tears shining in her eyes threaten to fall.

"It's the end of an era," Jasmine says. She has a tendency to be a little dramatic, but I can't help but agree with her.

Gabby's married. She's someone's *wife*. She has a husband. It's surreal to me, even though I've had nearly a year to get used to the idea of it.

Jasmine and Shelby hug her, and she turns to me last.

"Congratulations," I whisper as my arms slide around her. "Gabby Morgan-Wright."

She squeezes me as she lets out a laugh. It must be weird for her to hear her new name. The three of us follow her out the door, and she takes my hand as we walk down the stairs and into the living room where Ben is waiting for her. I hug him before I walk out the front door and past the waiting crowd of people, down the steps and to the edge of the driveway, just behind the car where Nate is standing. Jack comes out, a suitcase in either hand as he helps the driver load them into the trunk of the town car that's waiting. The door opens and Ben and Gabby walk out to applause and well wishes, hugging people as they gradually make their way to their ride. When they reach Nate and me, we all exchange hugs one more time before they disappear into the car.

I look around as I wait for them to drive away. Jack's arm is wrapped around Amy's shoulder, her head resting against his chest. Jessa's wrapped in her husband Ryan's arms, her back pressed against him and her sleeping daughter's head cradled in the crook of her neck. There's so much love in this family.

And then there's Nate and me.

The two of us are standing side by side, but we're a world apart.

Chapter SEVENTEEN

Long after all the guests have left and the house is quiet, I wander out to the porch and turn the fireplace on to its lowest setting, just to give me a little bit of warmth. I sit down on one of the wicker loveseats and watch the flames flicker and cast dancing shadows across the hearth. Confusion swirls around inside of me, making my stomach ache.

Once again, I have no idea what I'm doing. I left that hotel room a week ago thinking I'd seen the last of Nate. I was okay with that, I honestly was. It was nice to have a few hours of perfection without having to worry about the real world, about anything that was happening outside of that room. Then Fate, cruel bastard that it is, had to bring him back into my life. And now…now I'm not sure if that night is enough for me, knowing he wants more. But the thing is, I don't know if I'm all wrapped up in Nate or the *idea* of him. I'm scared of what would happen if I brought him into my very real life, which, let's face it, doesn't include a great track record when it comes to love. I don't think I know how to make it work, at least…not right now. I don't want to be hurt again, and the instinct for self-preservation overshadows my desire to just…be *with* him. I want him to be happy. I want him to have what his parents have, what his siblings have: real, deep, unwavering and unquestionable love. I want him to love and be loved by someone who can give him her whole heart without worrying about holding a part of it back for herself, just in case he breaks it.

He deserves so much more than what I can give him.

I'm pulled out of my thoughts by the sound of soft footfalls behind me. I know it's Nate, even without looking. I can *feel* his presence; the inexplicable way the atmosphere around me changes when he's near, the way he makes the air around me feel like it's buzzing. I turn toward him and my eyes lock with his. We stare at each other for a long moment, and it's like time just stops.

It takes everything in me to turn away from him, but only seconds later I hear his footsteps drawing near, my pulse quickening with every inch of distance that he closes between us. He steps in front of me, and when I look up I see that his duffel bag is slung over his shoulder. The sight of it makes my heart drop all the way down to my toes.

His eyes are so sad. The light that was there—the light that I loved seeing in them, the light that I sought out—is gone.

"You're leaving?" I ask, stating the obvious. My voice is shakier than I expected it would be.

Nate's eyebrows knit together, and he swallows as he nods slowly. "Yeah. My flight leaves early tomorrow, I'll just get a hotel room near the airport."

This completely unexpected spark of anger rips through me when I hear his words, and I can't control myself.

"Maybe stop by the bar?" It's a low blow, possibly the only thing I could say that would hurt him. I hate myself for even saying it; I'm not that petty and mean.

His eyes widen in shock, like I've just slapped him.

God, I'd give anything to take that back.

"That is so fucking unfair, Callie," he says, his voice gravely and low.

I tilt my head down to look at my fingers, which are all knotted up in my lap. I can't even look him in the eye. "I know," I say. I think back to the first night that we met, how I thought he was just some playboy looking to score. Knowing him the way I do now, it seems especially unfair that I've chosen to use that night against him. "That night when we met you said that you had never done something like that before, and you were so at ease. I thought…" I shake my head, wishing I hadn't said anything at all. This isn't going to help matters.

"So, you think this is an act for me, but…I'm just supposed to take your actions at face value?" he asks. I can see the anger simmering in his eyes, so cloudy and blue.

"I don't think it's an act. I shouldn't have said that, I don't know why I did."

"I know why you did." He's gripping the handle of his bag so tightly that his knuckles are white. Oh, how I want to reach out and soothe them.

"No you don't," I reply, even though I'm not entirely sure that he's wrong.

"I'm sorry Ethan cheated on you, Callie. And I'm sorry that you don't think you can trust me."

I think I can trust him, and that's precisely what my problem is. I've thought that so many times before, only to be let down. I don't say anything, because I have nothing to say, really.

"You want some kind of guarantee that I'm not Ethan, that I'm not an asshole. And you know what?" he says, raising his right arm in exasperation before it comes down and lands with a slap against the side of his thigh. He watches me with intent eyes, and I feel like he can see right through me, right to the heart of me. Like he can see everything that makes me who I am. If I were capable of doing such a thing, I almost think I'd shrink under his gaze. "I don't think you're scared of success or failure, of whether or not our relationship would work out. I think you're scared of *life*. I think you're scared of *living*."

"I'm scared of getting my heart broken again, Nate," I say, and that is very much true. But what I don't tell him is that I'm scared that my inability to fully commit might wind up breaking his. "You don't need to read into it more than that."

"What do you want me to tell you?" he says, completely ignoring the last part of what I just told him. His voice is getting a little louder, and he drops his bag to the ground with a loud thud. "Do you want me to tell you that I'm not that guy, Callie? That I won't do that? I could say those words a million times, but you wouldn't believe it, because you don't think you deserve someone who doesn't treat you like shit. Your dad left, Ethan cheated on you." He takes a deep breath and closes his eyes before they focus on me, all clear and blue and full of hurt. "You think that's what you get."

I stand up, pulled to my feet by the sudden rush of anger I'm feeling. I've known him one week and suddenly he thinks he's my therapist? "You don't know shit about me, Nate." I practically spit out the words, but even though I'm angry and rightfully so, they don't sound right when I say them. "How dare you throw that in my face."

For a moment that's so fleeting I almost think I imagined it, he looks completely wrecked. But he doesn't apologize; instead he takes a step forward, locking his eyes with mine. I couldn't look away even if I wanted to. "I know that you twirl your hair when you're nervous," he says, and all the anger I heard in his voice only seconds ago is completely gone. Everything about him now is just very soft. Gentle. Like the whole world hangs in the balance of this conversation. "I know that you hum off key, and that you don't realize the effect that you have on people…the effect you have on *me*. I know that you say my name in your sleep, and I know you want to change the world. I know that you've got a smile that just…" he trails off, pressing his lips together as he taps his fingers on his chest, right over his heart. "I know that I'm falling in love with you. And I know, I *know* that you're falling in love with me, too. And I know that we can spend the rest of our lives figuring out the rest."

When Nate finishes talking, he looks kind of stunned, like he just let everything spill out of him without even realizing that he did it.

I *am* stunned. *The rest of our lives* rings in my ears, filling me with dread. Breaking up with Ethan hurt me, there's no denying that. But Nate…it would be so much worse if I lost him. And I know that now, after only a week. How will I feel in a month? A year?

"It's not that simple," I say, trying so hard not to cry. I want him so badly, I just can't let myself have him. It's so easy to be idealistic when we're standing here thinking about forever. It would be different trying to make it work in the real world.

Nate reaches forward, and I'm surprised when his warm hand wraps around mine because the distance between us feels too great to be spanned by just a simple touch. The pad of his thumb brushes across my knuckles, and my eyelids flutter at the contact. "It is that simple," he says, looking down at our hands. "You're just trying to complicate things so it'll be easier for you to walk away from me. I know you're thinking of the what ifs, wondering if I'm just like him; if I'm charming you now just to hurt you later."

"I'm not thinking it," I say, my voice very quiet. "I'm scared of it."

"Maybe," Nate replies, sighing. "But I think you're really scared that I'm *not* like him. That I am who I say I am, that I can and will love you the way I say I will. That maybe this is it."

I look up at him, and the hope in his eyes nearly undoes me. "You've known me a week, Nate. How can you possibly know that?"

He shrugs, squeezing my hand. "I just do. What difference does it make how long we've known each other?"

Because it's crazy, I want to say. Instead, I take the easy way out. "Can't we just keep things the way they are?" I ask.

I can see the disappointment in his face; it's an immediate reaction the very second the words are out of my mouth. "What do you mean?"

"Just..." I can't bring myself to say the words, and I can't look him in the eye. I shrug and look down at the ground as his hand slips from mine. The air feels colder than it did just a second ago.

"Sex," he whispers, like it kills him to even say it. Like the word is... unfathomable.

I nod. I can't speak past the lump in my throat.

"I can't." He offers me a sad smile, like he wishes he could do it but it's just not in his genetic makeup. "Not with you."

"Not with me?"

He shakes his head. "I need more."

Tears well up in my eyes and I blink past them as I cross my arms over my chest, trying to keep out the chill. Of course I would find the one guy who turns down sex for love. That's the story of my pathetic life, and that's what makes the cynical part of me start running her mouth.

"What happens when it all goes to shit?" I ask.

Nate closes his eyes for a moment before he brings his hand up and cups my cheek. I lean into it, loving the way his rough palm is so gentle against my skin. I think this is the last time I'm going to feel it.

"Callie," he sighs. "What happens when it doesn't?"

I look at him for a long while, not really able to give him an answer. Not the one he wants, anyway. He's asking for my heart, and it's not whole enough to give to anyone yet. Maybe it never will be, I don't know.

"Please stay," I whisper. It's pathetic that I'm begging, but I've never felt desperation like this. It's my last night here and I want to be with him, even if we just stand like this all night, with his hand on my cheek as our only connection. I reach up and fiddle with one of the buttons on his shirt, and my forehead comes to rest against Nate's chest. It's the strangest sensation, feeling his muscles both tighten and relax at the same time. He brings his other hand up and runs his fingers through my hair.

"I can't stay," he says, pressing a kiss against the crown of my head, and I gather fistfuls of his shirt in my hands.

He pulls me close, cradling me against him as he buries his head in my neck. And I don't know when it happens, but suddenly his lips are on mine, very soft, very gentle. Very final. It's the sweetest, slowest, most tender kiss anyone's ever given me. It's the kind of kiss that makes me feel like my whole world is ending and beginning at the same time. He pulls away quickly, like he has to make himself do it, and he picks up his bag. He walks off the porch, stopping once to turn and look at me. It's then that I completely lose it, letting out some sad, strangled sound as I bring my hand up to my mouth to muffle my cries. This is it.

This is *it*.

I know Nate wants to come back and comfort me, but he can't. He looks like I feel: like his heart is breaking.

But he keeps walking.

Alone, into the dark.

Away from me.

Chapter
EIGHTEEN

I wake up to a soft rapping against the door and sit up, having to squint my tired eyes against the too-bright sunlight that's streaming through the windows.

"Callie?" The muffled voice belongs to Amy. It's soft and tentative, very motherly. Something about it makes tears well up in my eyes, and I'm surprised I have any tears left considering I cried myself to sleep last night. My entire face feels swollen and hot.

"Yeah?" I say, my voice all deep and raspy.

"Are you okay?"

"Yes, thank you. I'm all right." She's going to know that's a lie, but I guess I can't have everything.

"When you're ready, come on into the kitchen and I'll make you something to eat."

"Okay."

Despite how awful I feel, I really am hungry, so I shuffle into the bathroom and turn the faucet to as hot as I'll be able to tolerate. Steam fills the room before long, helping me clear my head. I step beneath the spray and let the water wash the past day away.

Even though I do my best not to think about Nate, the more I try to avoid it, the more my traitor mind conjures up the look on his face when he'd smile at me. The salty sweet taste of his skin, the way his lips felt when they were pressed against mine. The water washes away more tears as they fall, and I wonder how

I could've ever let him walk away? But...how could I have asked him to stay? Even now I can feel every broken part of me just barely hanging on, and if that's all I have to offer him, maybe this is all for the best. I worry that I'm going to vacillate over this decision for the rest of my life, long past the time when Nate will have moved on, and long past the time when I should have.

I don't even bother to dry my hair; at this point I'm too exhausted to care about what I look like. I pin it up in a loose bun and slip on my most comfortable clothes, then I walk out of my bedroom and make my way into the kitchen.

Amy's sitting at the table, writing in a red leather-bound journal. She looks up at me with a sympathetic expression, then closes her book and walks over to the coffee maker. She pours me a cup and sets it on the table, then she walks over and wraps her arms around me, enveloping me in the kind of hug that only a mother can give. Here come the tears again, only this time I don't try to stop them.

Amy lets me cry, gently rubbing soothing circles along my back. I just can't believe the kindness that seems to run in this family. I've hurt her son—she must know that I did—and yet here she is, comforting me.

"I'm sorry," I say, and it comes out like more of a cry than I intended it to.

She leans back a bit, bringing her hands to rest on my upper arms, giving them a gentle squeeze. "Oh, sweetie. What ever for?"

"For Nate."

Amy looks at me for a long while, her brows pulled together like she doesn't even know what I'm talking about. But she does know, I'm certain of it.

"He left early because we had a fight."

She smiles, looking down at the table. "That's not why he left," she says. "Without knowing you as well as I know my son, Callie, I'd venture a guess that you're both prone to rash decisions when it comes to protecting your heart."

I sit back in the chair, completely stunned. I try to find some words to tell her that she's wrong, but she's not. Even I can't deny that.

"Trust me, Callie. I don't pair people up, and I'm not a meddling mother. I want my children to find happiness on their own; I'll never try to force it on them, ever. I don't believe that you need to be in a relationship to be happy. And if *you*, Callie, are happy with your life the way it is, then that's wonderful. But I've seen the way that you look at my son, and I've seen the way he looks at you. There's something there, but you both have to want it. Being alone is great, but sharing your life with someone is great, too."

I swallow down past the painful lump in my throat, willing the words out of my mouth. "I was sharing my life with someone," I tell her, although I suspect she already knows this. "He turned out to be a person that I shouldn't have shared my life with."

She takes a deep breath, smiling as she sighs. "I think we've all been there."

I raise my eyebrows. "You have?" When I look at her and Jack together, it's difficult to believe that there was ever anyone else for either one of them.

"Absolutely."

I wrap my hands around the warm coffee cup in front of me, waiting for her to tell me her story.

"I suppose I should give you an anecdote about my past romantic failings, and somehow convince you that Nate's the most perfect man on the planet, that he'd never hurt you. My son is a good man, Callie. He could make anyone's life wonderful, but it's not my job to convince you to love him," she says, reaching out and taking my hand in hers. "Life offers no guarantees, so I can't offer them to you either. But when you meet someone you want to share your life with, the guarantees won't matter to you. You'll look at that person and know that being with them is worth the risk, and only then will you be willing to take it."

I nod, leaning forward and taking a sip of coffee, letting the warm liquid soothe my throat.

"You have a plane to catch in a few hours," she says, smiling. "And I told Gabby that I'd start planning our trip."

"Your trip to New York," I say, completely letting go of any notion that she'd still invite me to come along with them.

"*Our* trip to New York, Callie," she says patiently, like she absolutely refuses to let me have any angst over it.

"But what about-"

"It's going to be the three of us. You, me and Gabby. And you're going to have the time of your life regardless of who you're dating. Besides, you're not the kind of woman who lets a man ruin her fun, are you?"

I laugh and shake my head, even though I should correct her, because for far too long I have been exactly that kind of woman. Somehow, though, I have a feeling that I won't be for much longer.

Chapter
NINETEEN

*I*t's been three weeks since I've returned home from Virginia, and nearly everything about my hometown feels different to me since I've been back. It's too bright, it's too hot, it's too…everything. Something shifted in me while I was away, and I'm not sure if anything will ever be the way it used to be. Is that a good thing? Is it bad?

Regardless, it doesn't take me too long to get back into the bland, boring routine of my everyday life here. Every morning I wake up, turn on my computer, and I work until late in the evening. Some people (like Gabby) might call it avoidance, but I call it drive. The more clients I have, the more money I'll make. The more time I won't have to dwell on all the ways I know I'm messing up my life.

My mother comes home every night and makes me dinner like I'm still a child. I hate it, but I can't make myself leave. I'm stuck in this strange holding pattern that I can't get out of—or won't get out of—and it's the most uncomfortable and maddening thing I've ever experienced. I hang out with Ben and Gabby a few times after they get back from their honeymoon, and I can tell that they both want to call me out on my jackassery, but they're not quite willing to do that yet. Maybe there's a waiting period for calling your friend out on being an idiot. Because the more I think about it, the more I think maybe I was being—*am* being—an idiot when it comes to him.

When it comes to *Nate*. I don't really let myself think of his name that often, because those four letters are what seems to send me into a tailspin of self-pity.

Not the thought of his beautiful, smiling face. Not the thought of the way he touched me. Just his name.

It's not until my mother catches me looking at the wedding photos that Gabby emailed me earlier in the day that she finally broaches the subject. She knows something's been bothering me since I've been back, and she's enough of a mind-reader that she probably knows it's a guy. She's always been over-the-top with her motherly intuition, which is completely maddening (and helpful) at times.

It's a candid shot that does me in, one of me and Nate dancing, smiling at each other. He'd just said something funny—I can't remember what it was—and I was looking at him like he was my sun, moon and stars. If I wasn't one of the people in that photo, I would've guessed the two of them were very much in love. Maybe we are, and I just need to let myself feel it, I don't know. What I do know is that looking at this picture makes my chest ache, makes it difficult for me to breathe. I had him right there within reach, and then I willingly let go.

"Is that him?" Mom asks, casually swiping a dishtowel across the kitchen counter.

"Who?" I reply, no doubt setting off her overactive bullshit detector.

She sighs. "The one who's got you looking like the world stopped making sense."

"He's not the one who made me look like this," I tell her. My mother looks at me in a way that is uniquely hers. She knows me as only a mother can; she can see all the little idiosyncrasies that make me…well, me. She knows me right down to my bones, which makes hiding things from her particularly impossible, but I'm telling her the truth this time. "I'm the one who made myself look like this, Mom, although he does have something to do with it."

She tosses the dishtowel on the counter, pulls out the chair next to mine, and sits down.

"His name is Nate," I tell her.

That's all I say, and my mom's eyes widen, waiting for more information. Information that I'm not sure I want to give to her. "How'd you meet?"

Of course she'd ask me that. Of course she would.

I sigh. "I don't want to tell you that." I realize immediately that I should've just made up a story, but I can't lie to her. I never could.

"Why not?"

The question hangs in the air around us for a few seconds before I finally answer. "Because I'm afraid you'll think less of me."

"Impossible." She says that word with such conviction that I'm sure she's right.

"I met him at the airport on my way to Gabby's wedding. There was a weather delay, and we…spent it together." I don't really want to elaborate, but my mom's a smart woman; she understands what it is that I'm not telling her.

"Oh."

"I didn't think I'd see him again, which…yeah, I guess doesn't make this sound any better. I just…I wanted to put something, *someone* between Ethan and me."

Mom nods slowly, taking all of this in. "Why was he at the wedding?"

"Turns out he's Ben's brother."

Mom's not as shocked about this development as I would've thought she'd be. Instead of offering me a reply, she just looks at the picture, and a soft smile pulls at her lips. "You love him," she says.

"I only knew him a week." I don't even try to deny what she said, because what's the point?

"If you feel it, you feel it, Cal," she says, squeezing my hand. "What difference does it make how long it takes?"

"Nate said the exact same thing."

"He sounds like a smart guy," she replies, smiling.

"How can I trust it?" I ask.

"Why is a love you feel right away more trustworthy than the one that takes time to grow?"

"Because that love is rooted in something," I tell her. "I wouldn't be worried about waking up one morning and not feeling it anymore."

"Love is love, Cal. It's not about how long it takes you to feel it, it's about how much effort you put into it to make it last. Don't act like it's something that just happens. It's something that you have to nurture."

I sit back in my chair and think about what she just said. My relationship with Ethan fell apart because he wasn't willing to nurture what we had. If I'm honest with myself, it started to die long before the cheating. But did I nurture it, or did I treat it like something that was just a given once it happened? I liked being with him, I put effort into that, but what did I do to make our love grow? Did I do anything to give it roots? I had list of things that I thought should happen once Ethan and I started dating. We'd get serious, move in together, get married, have children, and then spend the rest of our lives together. But I wasn't really investing in a life with him, I was checking off a list. I'm not to blame for the way the relationship ended, but I am to blame for not putting more into it. Although now I'm beginning to realize that may be a blessing in disguise.

Maybe Nate was right. Maybe I needed to be with a person who didn't fit in order to learn the lessons I needed to learn to find the person who does fit.

"I barely know him," I say, voicing the one niggling concern that pulls at me, stops that bud of feelings I have for Nate from fully blossoming.

"So get to know him," Mom says like it's the simplest thing in the world. Maybe it is.

"Is that what you did with my father?" I ask.

Mom knows exactly what I'm getting at.

"Your father was an adventure," she says a bit wistfully.

"An ugly one."

Removing her hand from mine, she reaches over and touches my cheek. "Not so much."

"You don't regret it?" I ask, wondering how she possibly couldn't. He left us alone, how could she not hate him for that?

"Not for a second," she replies. "It was a learning experience. Besides, he gave me you."

I swallow, somehow managing a smile. "But you're alone."

Mom stands, then leans down and kisses my forehead, cupping my cheeks with her hands. "I love you so much," she says, smiling softly. "But when something bad happens, you retreat. You don't give it another go, and that scares me. I'm worried that one day you'll wake up all alone, regretting that you pushed people away and regretting the things you never did because you were afraid. We all fall down, we all fail. The strong ones get back up, and they try again. I raised a strong one."

"Mom-"

"You only get one life," she says, interrupting me. "You have to fill it up with all the love and laughter that you can. Run away from those things long enough and you'll forget how to find them. I'm alone because I'm happy being alone. If you're happy the way things are now, then keep being happy." She looks over at the pic of Nate and me that's still up on my laptop screen. "If you're not happy, then chase that happiness. If you think you can find some of it with him, then do it. Life's too short to deny yourself love, Callista."

I close my eyes and let her words sink in.

She's right. I know she's right.

"I've got my sunscreen, my bikini, and my English-to-Greek phrase book. Saturday can't get here fast enough," Jasmine says, stretching her legs out in front of her as she leans back into the soft green grass. She, Gabby and I are eating lunch at one of our favorite parks, and the weather is perfect. The sun is shining and the breeze is warm; it's enough to help a girl forget her troubles for an hour or two. The talk I had with my mother last night has been weighing on my mind all morning, pushing me to the brink of action. I'm just not sure exactly what to do now. Do I call Nate? It seems like the logical next step, but it also doesn't seem like it's enough.

"I don't think you realize how long that flight's going to be," Gabby says, licking a dollop of mustard off the tip of her thumb. "It's going to be the longest flight of your life."

I look at Jasmine, who's looking at me, and I know she's thinking the same thing that I am. How long of a grace period does Gabby get to talk about her honeymoon before we all put a stop to it?

"Go to Europe once, and suddenly you're a flight time expert," I say, winking at her to let her know I'm teasing.

Gabby swats at me, laughing. "I'm sorry, I'll stop talking about it soon."

"You get another three days, and then we're cutting you off," I tell her.

"Be glad Callie's your best friend. I'd cut you off two weeks ago."

Gabby laughs, throwing a balled-up napkin at Jasmine as she stands up and brushes off the back of her skirt.

"I've got to get back to the office," Jasmine says, gathering her trash into a plastic grocery bag. "I'm going to stress myself out to get ready for the vacation that's supposed to de-stress me, so that's fun."

I sigh loudly. "Ah, being your own boss has its perks."

"So does having company subsidized healthcare," Jasmine replies with a wink. "I'll see you ladies later."

"Have a fun trip!" I yell after her.

She turns towards us, walking backwards as she holds out her arms. "You know I will!"

Gabby and I stand up, and I walk with her to the corner of the park, the one closest to her office.

"Hey," I say, sounding more nervous than I actually feel, which surprises me. "I was wondering if you would feel comfortable giving me Nate's number."

Her eyes widen, caught somewhere between surprise and happiness. "You don't already have it?"

I shake my head. "I didn't think it would be a good idea," I admit.

"But…" she says as she digs in her purse, pulling out a pad of paper and a pencil.

"But I'd like to talk to him."

"About what?"

She's so damn nosy.

"About things," I tell her. Partly because I'm not yet sure what exactly it is that I want to say to him, and partly because whatever it is that I do say, I think he should be the first person to hear it.

Thankfully, she doesn't press the issue. She just grins at me as she hands me the piece of paper with his number written on it. "He asks about you, you know."

I wander through the park after lunch, walking across the soccer field and over toward the playground. There's something about the light laugher of the children on the swing sets that helps put me at ease, helps me focus my thoughts. I take a seat on a bench nearby, settling in against its forest-green slats. It's cool here in the shade, beneath this elm tree's long, sturdy branches. It reminds me of the trees in Virginia, which makes me think of Nate.

I sigh. *Nate.*

My mom told me yesterday that if I'm happy with the way my life is that I should keep doing what I'm doing. I'm fully ready to admit to myself now that I'm not happy, not by a long shot. And it's not just that I'm not happy, it's that I'm keeping myself from being happy by holding onto the past. By making excuses for myself. By not taking chances.

My life now consists of standing on the sidelines, in the safe zone, watching people live their lives. I've reduced myself to a casual observer of the world instead of an active participant in it. It's true that not taking risks saves me from feeling the pain of failure, but it prevents me from feeling the joy of simply being alive. I realize now that I *need* Nate in my life. And it's not because I'm lonely, and it's not because I can't survive without him. It's because he makes me want to do all the things that I'm afraid of, and become all the things that I'm not, but that I desperately wish I could be. He makes me want to open my arms, take a deep breath and appreciate the beauty in the world. What more could I possibly ask from a person? A broken heart seems like a small price to pay in return for the possibility of a lifetime full of love and happiness.

Now I'm afraid that I may have lost Nate without ever really having him in the first place. I haven't spoken to him since he left the night of the wedding. Even though Gabby said that he's asked about me, I can't deny that it stings that he hasn't tried to contact me. I'm fully aware of what a hypocrite that makes me, thank you very much. I take a look at the number scrawled across the bright-pink sticky note I'm holding in my hand, and the sight of the numbers makes my heart thunder in my chest. All I need to do is dial these numbers, and I can hear is voice. All I need to do is dial these numbers, and I can tell him how I feel. These numbers could lead to so many wonderful things…why are they so scary?

I reach into my gigantic mess of a bag, nearly elbow-deep, fishing for my phone. The sharp edge of something catches the inside of my wrist, and I wrap my fingers around it, wondering what exactly it could be. When I pull my hand out of my bag, I can't believe my eyes.

It's a single-serving box of Raisin Bran, with a note taped to the back. Underneath an address it reads:

For a healthy heart.

It's from Nate, who always seems to know exactly what I need when I need it. I've spent the past three weeks wondering how I could fall in love with him so quickly, and now all I can think is…how could I not?

I blink through the tears in my eyes, my heart feeling more intact than it has in ages and so full I almost think I can't take it. It's then that I look up, right above the bench I'm sitting on, and I see a plain blue sign with white lettering. I turn, gripping the back of the bench to give me leverage while I read it.

This playground donated and maintained by Bryson Interiors

I designed their website two years ago when they were on the brink of going out of business, and now they've sponsored a park. Business is booming now, so I guess I can take some small sliver of credit for the fun the kids are having on the swing set twenty feet away. Maybe I have something to do with the smiles on their faces.

I'm not curing cancer, but I am leaving my fingerprint on this world, starting with a tiny playground in a tiny park in the middle of Dallas. And Nate was right, that is something. It's fitting, I suppose, that I'd feel so close to him when I'm so far away, considering I'd done everything I could to put distance between us while we were together.

I get it, universe. I get it.

A phone call isn't enough, this requires a risk.

I'm finally willing to take one.

I make it home in record time, then sprint into my room and throw heaps of clothing into my suitcase. I'm not even paying a bit of attention to anything I'm putting in there, but I don't care, I don't care. I scribble out a note for my mother on the back of an old envelope, hop in my car, and start driving.

Chapter TWENTY

*R*oughly eighteen hours after I leave Dallas, I'm standing on the curb in front of Nate's house in Boulder. It doesn't look at all like I expected, not that he ever told me what his house looked like anyway. It's a Craftsman style, with dark brown siding and white shutters. The lawn is impeccably landscaped, with lush green grass and well-trimmed bushes. The trees are just starting to show a hint of fall, the edges of the leaves showing a tinge of color with muted reds and washed-out yellows. I bet they'll look like they've caught fire in a few weeks, and I feel the beginnings of a dull ache in my chest because I want to be here to see that.

I look down at the address on the note that Nate taped to the cereal box he left in my bag, then I glance up at the numbers that are all lined up in a perfect row on the awning over the porch. This is the street and this is definitely the house. There's a grey Jeep parked in the driveway, it's shiny paint is streaked with caked-on dried mud. I'm guessing it belongs to Nate and has probably seen more death-defying adventures than I'd care to know about.

There hasn't been even the slightest hint of nervousness since I hopped in my car and pulled out onto the interstate, but now that I'm here I think maybe my heart is going to beat right out of my chest. I feel like I should've called, like maybe it's not fair to just show up here like this, even though he did basically leave me an invitation to do just this. Ugh, I can stand here and debate over it for the rest of the night, or I could just work up the nerve to walk up the steps and knock on his door. What do I have to lose? Nothing I haven't lost already.

I take a deep breath and slowly exhale, closing my eyes as I feel the slightest bit of relaxation tug at the dull edges of my overstimulated nerves. I'm taking a chance; chances don't feel safe, Callie, they feel…well, they feel exactly like this. I didn't drive all this way to check out the real estate in Nate's neighborhood, so it's time for me to make a move. To make a move and see if this crazy road trip thing was a good idea or a really, really bad one. I move myself forward, get some momentum going, and walk up to his front door.

As soon as I raise my hand to knock, the door flies open. My heart slips and falls when I look up into a face that doesn't belong to Nate.

"Can I help you?" Now *this* is exactly the kind of guy I would picture when I thought of people who lived in Colorado. Shelby would probably describe him as 'crunchy.' He's you're typical tree-hugging, granola-loving hippie type. His hair is a bit shaggy, but he has a nice smile and a friendly face.

"I'm sorry," I say, a little flustered. "I was just here to visit…" A friend? I'm not exactly sure what to say here, although 'Is Nate here?' would probably work, I can't seem to get myself to say it. "I came looking for-"

"You're Callie," he says with a knowing smile. Never before has the simple sound of my name made me feel so reassured and welcome. He delivers what I can only describe as an instant calm.

"I am." I smile back at him. "I'm here to see-"

"Nate," we both say at the same time. We laugh together too, a nervous and awkward sound.

"I'm sorry, this is creepy, I'm…I'm being creepy," Nate's friend says, stepping forward and shaking my hand. "I'm Kevin."

"Hi. How do you know my name?"

"Oh, Nate, he talks about you. A lot."

I can't help the warm rush of satisfaction that rushes through me. He talks about me. That's good, right? Yikes, what if it's not. "Does he say good things or bad?"

Kevin doesn't reply, he just looks at me for a few seconds. "You know, he's actually not here right now." My stomach drops, and I automatically assume that not only has he been saying bad things, but he's also given his friend pre-emptive instructions to get me the hell out of here.

"Oh, okay," I say, turning around to walk back to my car. I'll just have to figure out a new game plan. Find a hotel maybe, and give him a call.

"Wait, no." He reaches out for me, touching my elbow before I make my way down the stairs. "He's really not here, I'm not feeding you a line. I just stopped by to borrow some trunks." He points down at the orange shorts he's wearing.

"I'll come back later."

He laughs at me in a totally dismissive, yet friendly way. "If he finds out that you were here and I let you leave, he'd beat my ass. There's a lake a few blocks from here." He shuts the door behind him and reaches for a towel that's hanging off the porch railing, then flings it over his shoulder. "Feel like taking a walk?"

*K*evin leads me through a small clearing, and for a fleeting moment I begin to wonder if walking through the woods with a stranger was the best course of action here. My brain is working overtime, because if anyone would get murdered after finally deciding to try to get over their commitment issues, it would be me. As soon as I decide that I should probably turn and run the other way, Kevin pulls back a huge, leafy tree branch to reveal a lake surrounded by lush trees just starting to change colors. I can hear the laughing voices of the people in the water, but I can't see them.

I can't see them because Kevin and I are standing on what I can only describe as a cliff, which is pretty much my worst nightmare come to life.

Let me amend my previous thought: if anyone would die from jumping off a cliff in order to get to the love of their life after finally deciding to get over their commitment issues, it would be me.

"Is there another way down?" I ask, twirling the ends of my hair around my finger.

Kevin turns and smirks at me, like he was expecting the question. "Yeah, but it takes a while to get down there, and you have to take a different path."

We're only about twenty feet up, but it might as well be a mile. My heart is beating triple-time, my fight or flight response is gearing up and ready to go.

"Isn't that water freezing?" I'm desperate for any kind of excuse to actually stick here. If I didn't want to see Nate so badly, I'd ask this hippie to show me that different path immediately, if not sooner.

Kevin shakes his head. "It's not too bad. This is probably the last semi-warm day we'll have here for a while, so we've got to enjoy the water while we can." He balls up his towel and tosses it off to the left, where it gets snagged on a tree branch, just dangling above the water, mocking him.

I let out a quiet laugh, but he doesn't seem to hear me over the laughter of his friends in the water, razzing him for missing the beach. I mean, really, there's one tree in his way and he manages to get the towel stuck on it.

"Jesus, Mitchell. Did you have to take my favorite pair? When I said you could borrow some shorts, I meant for you to take one of the pairs that I hate." It's Nate. I never thought I'd be so happy to hear another person's voice, especially when they were yelling up at a cliff while treading in icky brown lake water.

Kevin shrugs, then he leans forward to yell. "Hey, I can't help it if we both have impeccable taste. Speaking of," he says, looking back at me. "There's someone here to see you."

I expect Nate to say something in response, but he doesn't. There's nothing but quiet. Seconds of it. An eternity of it.

"C'mere," Kevin says, offering me an encouraging smile. I take a few steps forward until I can see over the edge of the cliff, the guys in the water slowly coming into view. All of them are staring up at me, but Nate's is the only face I see. He's surprised, but slowly, a smile spreads across his lips. It's a smile that makes me feel light, because if I had any doubt that I did the right thing by driving here, all that doubt has just been erased.

"Callie?" he says, like he can't believe it's really me.

"Hi." I give him a little nervous half-wave.

"What are you doing here?" He doesn't sound angry, just shocked.

"I wanted to talk to you, but I didn't have your number, so I thought I'd stop by, because I need to tell you something."

"So tell me," he shouts, smiling.

"I didn't really expect to have to yell it in front of a bunch of strangers."

"These are my friends," he says, like that means anything to me.

"Okay?"

"You can jump down here and tell me if you want." He wants to laugh, the beautiful jerk.

"You're really going to make this difficult for me, aren't you?"

"Just a little bit."

I take a deep breath. Better just get this over with.

"You scared me, Nate."

"I scared you?"

"Yes!"

He laughs, I can hear it echoing against the trees. "Why?"

"You make falling in love seem easy, and I was scared that it wouldn't last." Terrified is probably the more appropriate word, but it seems like a little too much for this moment.

"You're not scared now?"

"More scared than I've ever been. But I don't care. It doesn't seem to matter that much anymore."

"And what happens when it goes to shit?" he asks. I asked him the very same thing the night he left me standing on the porch of his parents' house in Virginia. The night that started me down the path that would lead me here. I've spent weeks stewing over everything that happened that evening, but now that I'm here and so close to Nate, I can't bring myself to regret any of it. And if he wants me to refute every single fear I voiced during that argument, I'll do it. I'm not going to let any of those things come between us anymore.

So, I reply with the very same thing he said to me that night. "What happens when it doesn't?"

Nate smiles, and I think it's the most beautiful thing I've ever seen. The three weeks of misery and an eighteen-hour drive were worth it just to see it again. "What now?"

I shrug. "I was kind of hoping we could talk without yelling," I say, laughing.

"I have a lot more I need to say."

"I was kind of hoping I could kiss you."

I feel the blush creep up into my cheeks, warm against the cool wind. "That sounds like a good plan."

"You have to come down here first."

I'd rappel down a mountain to be with him at this point, but that doesn't mean that I'm not still a little wary. "Are there eels?"

A nod and a grin. "Tons of them."

Only now do I realize that Nate's the only one in the water. Kevin's gone too, I have no idea where. I guess they all left to give us some privacy, even though we're practically yelling at each other across a body of water. And then, of course, there are the eels. Oh, well. What does it matter? I'd jump into a river full of them if it meant I'd get to be with Nate. So I walk right to the edge of that cliff and take a deep breath.

Then, I jump.

*W*e're sitting on the shore of the lake, looking out at the sunset over the rippling water. Nate's got a little fire going, but I don't really need it. It's warm enough being wrapped in his arms. I'm sort of halfway sprawled across his lap, my head resting in the crook of his neck, his towel wrapped around me. My clothes are wet and drying by the fire, so all I'm wearing now is one of Nate's t-shirts. Thankfully he walked to the lake wearing one, when I know his shirtlessness makes the world a more beautiful place.

"I was wondering how long it would take you to get here," Nate says as he kisses my shoulder, the gentle brush of his mouth making me shiver.

I know he's talking about a metaphorical journey, so I can't really find it in me to apologize. Three weeks is nothing; it could've taken me years to get to the point where I was ready to be with him.

"I was also worried that you'd never find that damn cereal box."

I laugh, lacing our fingers together. Holding his hand is one of my favorite feelings.

"I met Gabby and Jasmine at a park for lunch yesterday. I had already made up my mind that I wanted to talk to you, I knew that if I shut you out forever I would regret it. I was miserable without you, Nate, I was thinking about you all the time. I realized how stupid I was being, trading one form of misery because I had the potential to feel another. Why make myself unhappy in order to avoid something that I wasn't sure would ever happen in the first place? At least if something does happen..." If we break up, I want to say, but I don't want to jinx it. "I'll have gotten the chance to be happy. I don't want to miss out on that; it would be one of the biggest regrets of my life."

Nate's quiet, so I look up and he's gazing down at me with an expression that I can only describe as being full of love. How did I ever doubt, for one second, that this is exactly the place that I belong, that he's the person that I belong with?

"Anyway," I say, sighing. "We were at this park, and after lunch was over, I was sitting on a bench and I looked up and saw a sign that read that the playground there had been donated by this client of mine, and I thought back to what you said to me that day we were on the river, about making a difference in the world no matter how small it is," I say, gripping his fingers tightly. "You make me see everything differently. You quiet the cynic inside of me and make me believe there's so much more to life. And yesterday, I just wanted to talk to you; I've never wanted to talk to someone so badly, but...it wouldn't have been enough."

Nate's arms wrap around me a little tighter, and I feel myself relax against the heat of his body. It feels so good, so freeing to get all of this out, to have it in the open between us once and for all.

"I'm sorry about the way I left that night," he says. "I need to apologize for that."

"No you don't," I tell him.

He runs his palm across my thigh, just because. "I do, Callie. You were very straightforward about what you wanted from the get-go. I just...being with you, I couldn't help but want more. And I don't want you to think that I deal with my problems by running away from them, because I don't."

"I know," I tell him, punctuating the sentiment with a soft kiss. He brings his head down until our foreheads are touching.

"I just knew that if I stayed I'd wind up messing things up."

"What do you mean?" I ask. If anyone was going to mess anything up, it was going to be me.

"You needed some space to figure things out. If I had stayed that night, I don't know if I would've given it to you. I knew it would be best for me to get some distance from the situation, and I thought—I hoped—that when you were ready, *if* you were ever ready, I'd hear from you when you found that box."

"What if I hadn't ever found it?" Not that I really want to know the answer, but exploring possibilities is less sad and scary when you've already made your choice.

"With that bag of yours, it's entirely possible," he says laughing.

I playfully smack his arm. "It's not that big!"

"But it is that messy," he says, rocking me a little. "If you hadn't found it, I probably would've eventually asked Gabby to arrange some kind of party or something so we could bump into each other."

When I turn my head and look at him, I love the wry smile on his face. We're both thinking the same thing.

"You wouldn't have had to ask," I tell him, laughing. Gabby would've been all over that without Nate ever bringing it up. She was probably planning said party when we were eating lunch yesterday. "I'm glad I found it. Doing something like that, it was so *you*. Even if I hadn't found it, even if you hadn't left me something like that, I would've come looking for you. I knew I would do that eventually, even when you left. I just wasn't ready to accept it yet, if that makes any sense."

"It makes sense."

I bring his hand to my lips, and place a kiss on his knuckles. "You make me happy and hopeful in a way that I didn't think I'd ever feel again," I admit. He does so much more for me than that, but I have so much time to tell him those things.

Nate brushes his cheek against our clasped hands. "You make it easier for me to breathe. I just want you, Callie. Just you."

I snuggle against his chest, turning my head toward his heart. "You have me."

Nate and I walk along a dirt path that leads back to his house. My clothes are mostly dry, but I only slipped on my pants, not feeling quite comfortable enough to walk through his neighborhood just wearing his shirt and my shoes. My own shirt and the towel we'd been sharing are draped over Nate's right arm. His left arm is wrapped around my shoulder, pulling me close to his side.

The walk is pleasant; the air is fresh and cool and the crickets are chirping. It's a beautiful night made even more beautiful because of the man beside me. When we finally make it to his house, Nate pushes open the back gate, locking it behind us. He puts his hand on the small of my back as he leads me up the stairs to the back porch. The rickety old slats creak as we walk across them.

"I'm going to replace this in the spring," he says.

"The wood?"

"The whole thing. I'm going to build it out a bit, so there's room for a grill and a table, a place to have a little get together."

"I think that'll be nice," I say as he reaches for the screen door's handle.

I step over the threshold and into the kitchen. Even though I knew that Nate has been fixing the place up, I'm surprised by how nice it is in here. I'm not sure why I half-expected him to have questionable taste, just because he's a single guy. There are pristine cherry cabinets, stainless steel appliances, beautiful granite countertops. It's nice but kind of sterile, and not very Nate. The place doesn't have any personal touches; it doesn't look lived in.

This house *smells* like him though, like his arms are wrapped around me and my face is buried in his neck. I close my eyes and take a deep, deep breath.

"You did all this?" I ask, turning to my right and splaying my hands out on top of the granite.

Nate walks up behind me, pressing his chest against my back. I gasp, not really expecting that from him, but I relax into him seconds later. He pushes my hair to the side—over my shoulder—giving him access to my neck, where he kisses and licks his way across my skin. I've missed this feeling so much. And he's hard already, I can feel it. Unfortunately for him I'm in the mood to tease him tonight.

"Mmm-hmm," he hums, the vibration tickling my ear, making me shiver.

He lifts his shirt off of me and throws it onto the floor; then he wraps his arms around my waist, slipping his hand beneath the waistband of my pants. I don't have any underwear on; I'd taken them off to dry by the fire. I suck in a deep breath at the ticklish sensation his fingers leave in their wake, then he slides them down, down between my legs until I gasp.

"You need some-" my breath hitches, "accessories in here," I manage to say, kind of panting. This is moving a little faster than I intended it to, which...I don't know what I expected because we haven't seen each other in three weeks. Nate reaches around and gently rolls my nipple between his fingers as he simultaneously pulls me back against him, my ass grinding into his erection. I give it a little shake for retribution.

"Fuck," he sighs, his breath hot on my shoulder as he peppers kisses there.

"Don't worry," I say breathlessly, pretending he's talking about kitchen decor. "I'll help you pick out some things."

I turn around and stand on my tiptoes, making me just tall enough to reach his lips when he dips his head. I pull him close, pressing my bare chest to his, enjoying the little noises he makes as we kiss. The teasing part of my plan is quickly disintegrating, so I pull away from him, eliciting a groan.

"Show me more," I say, leading him into the next room. I walk backwards through the door, making sure Nate gets a good view of my chest while I stay just out of his reach.

We walk into the living room-slash-dining room, which is just as nice as the kitchen with its impeccable paint and glossy hardwood floors. But again, there's nothing Nate about the place. "This is nice," I say kindly. "But you need a throw on your sofa to break up all of that color. And you need some pictures. Lots of pictures."

Nate could not give a shit about what I'm telling him right now, but he plays along anyway. "Pictures of us," he says, firmly gripping my hips and picking me up. I wrap my arms around his neck and my legs around his waist, then kiss every inch of skin I can get my lips on. Screw the teasing, just...screw it.

I'm only aware that Nate's walking because I feel a breeze on my back as we move, but soon enough I'm pressed against a wall, and the look in Nate's eyes is straight-up predatory. He slides his hands up the insides of my arms, pinning my wrists above my head. Then his mouth and tongue are on my breasts, and my head clunks back against the wall.

"Do you..." Kiss. "Like..." Lick. "The paint?"

My head lolls to the side, because what color is this paint again? Oh yeah, blue. Placing my hands just above his ears, I tilt his head up and capture his mouth with mine. "Yes," I tell him between kisses. "It reminds me of your eyes."

He leans back, looking kind of surprised.

"It does," I say, tracing the line of his jaw with my fingertip. "I love your eyes."

He smiles softly, and I can't help but kiss those lips. Those beautiful, soft, perfect lips. It's deeper than I expected, needier, and when I pull away, Nate pulls my bottom lip through his teeth. I slide down his body a little, bucking my hips into his when I feel the hardness there, making him grunt. Once my feet are on the floor, I walk over to the staircase.

"Is the bedroom up here?" I ask.

He nods, somehow managing to make that simple gesture look sexy as hell.

I take the first few steps alone, sliding my hand along the bannister. "You need some light in here," I tell him, stopping to look at the beautiful paisley pattern that decorates the throw rug on the landing of the stairs. He closes the distance between us quickly—he must take two or three steps at a time—and the next thing I know he's gripping my waist and turning my body, bringing me down so that I'm sitting on the step just before the landing. He pulls off one shoe and then the other, tossing them away. They make loud 'thunks' as they bounce down the steps.

He slowly tugs on the cuffs of my pants until they slide off my thighs and down my calves, slipping off of my ankles. He throws those down the steps, too. Then he kneels before me a few steps down, spreading my legs. He buries his head between my thighs, licking me like he's been waiting his whole life to do it, like he just can't get enough. And I love it when he does this, I really do. It's difficult to tell him no and I'm crazy to do it, but I need more than this right now. I need *him*, no more teasing.

"Nate," I say softly, and he knows something is different by the tone of my voice. I skim my fingers through his hair, bringing my hand to rest just above his ear. He looks at me, his hands still. "I want you. I want to be with you, can we just..."

"Yeah," he replies, understanding. He moves so he's kind of leaning over me, and he presses his lips against my shoulder. "Yeah."

Afraid that I've taken us out of the moment, I wrap my arm around his neck and bring him down for a slow, tender kiss.

When we part, Nate sighs, breathing heavily. "Yeah, let's definitely do more of that." He picks me up and carries me up the steps, laving his tongue against every inch of skin he can reach. Once he lays me on his soft bed, he slides his shorts down his hips and I take a moment to appreciate him like this. Bare and vulnerable. Beautiful. Mine.

He kneels on the bed, lifting my legs until the bottoms of my feet come to rest against his chest. It reminds me a bit of the first night we were together, but everything is different now. Everything is better now, because this…this is the beginning of our lives together. His palms glide down my thighs, his fingertips are feather-light and ticklish; I can't help but laugh.

"Do that again," he says, smiling. It's a dopey, love-struck kind of smile. I wish I could take a picture of it and put it in my wallet.

"What?"

"Laugh, it's-"

"You want me to laugh?"

He looks bashful. "Yeah. It makes me…I don't know, just do it again."

I do laugh this time, and it's a real one, mainly because I don't know what he's getting at.

He must sense my confusion, because he says, "I like your voice." He shrugs, and it's kind of sweet how innocent he looks, despite the fact that he's stark naked.

"Nate," I say, reaching out for him and tangling our fingers together. I pull him down, but he holds his weight above me. "I love you." If he likes my voice, I can't think of nicer, truer words for him to hear it say.

"I love you so much," he replies, just breathing the words on my skin, like they'll become a part of me that way.

I smile, cradling the back of his head, and he pushes into me slowly, just watching me for a few seconds like he always does. He begins to move when I buck my hips, and for a few seconds we just kind of drift away together. I've never felt anything like him before, and I don't just mean this. I mean *him*. Everything about him. The weight of his gaze, the way his words sink right into my skin and take hold of my heart. Everything about him feels so perfect. So permanent.

I gently nudge Nate's shoulder and he rolls onto his back. I swing my leg over until I'm straddling his hips, then I sink down onto him, grinding against him, watching the way his eyelids flutter shut and his breathing picks up because we feel so, *so* good together. Pure pleasure is building up inside of me, radiating from pretty much every part of my body, almost indistinguishable from the rush of love that I feel for this man. I'm just all blissed out, light and airy, all warmth and anticipation.

I clasp Nate's hands in mine and lean forward, pressing my body against his.

"Hold onto me," Nate says, his voice raspy as he sits up. He slides his hands down my back and along my thighs, positioning me so that I'm sitting on him, my legs wrapped around him, so tight. There's not an inch of air between us, but he's still too far away. I want to be close enough to be a part of him. I want my name to be written on every cell in his body. Our chests are pressed together and it almost hurts to breathe, but it's still. Too. Far.

We rock against one another and Nate's hands are splayed across my back, anchoring me to him. Tighter, I want to tell him. Hold me tighter. I want his fingertips branded into my skin. His cheek is pressed against mine and his stubble is rough, but I want more. *More.*

"I can't get close enough," he says, his voice muffled as he presses his mouth to my neck. "To you, I…"

"Shhh," I whisper. "I'm here, I'm right here." I kiss the salty sheen from his skin, holding on for dear life as everything inside of me coils up and springs open, over and over, leaving me boneless and breathless. Nate isn't far behind me, letting out this strangled moan as his orgasm washes over him and my name falls from his lips. We hold each other as we come down, his hands tangled in my hair and mine drawing lazy patterns on his back. It's nice just holding each other, just being.

Eventually we collapse on the bed, our arms wrapped around each other as we doze off, exhausted from pretty much everything that's happened today.

I wake up in his arms a few hours later. It's dark outside, but the bedside lamp is on, casting a dull light across the room. Nate must've turned that on at some point after I fell asleep. For the first time since I've been here, I get a good look at this room. It's a lot like his room in Virginia; same colors, same earthiness. More photos of waterfalls and rivers, of mountains and ski slopes. Maybe it's a reminder of home? I notice there's a photo on the nightstand, on the far side of the bed. Careful not to wake him, I reach over and pick it up. As I snuggle up against his chest, I hold the picture above me because I just can't take my eyes off of it.

It's the photo of the two of us dancing at the wedding. The same one I couldn't stop looking at on my laptop. There's something sweet and comforting knowing that he liked it enough to get a print of it. That it meant enough to him to put it next to his bed.

"That one's my favorite," he says, sliding his fingertips across my upper arm.

I turn my head and look up at him, smiling. "Mine too."

He reaches out and presses the edge between his index finger and thumb. "Maybe I should frame it and put it downstairs."

"No," I say thoughtfully, placing it back on the nightstand. "I think it belongs up here."

He sighs. "Okay," he replies, and I can hear the smile in his voice. "So, I've never had redecoration foreplay before, but I guess there's a first time for everything."

I giggle as I brush my lips across the skin above his heart. "I think we'll have a lot of firsts together. Foreplay aside, this place could use a feminine touch." I gasp almost immediately, totally not meaning to imply the thing that I just implied. That *I* should be the feminine touch. "I didn't mean-"

Nate presses his finger against my lips. "Don't. I was kind of hoping you'd stay."

"I brought a few weeks' worth of clothes. At least I think I did, I was in kind of a hurry when I packed."

"We can get you new clothes," he says, twirling a strand of my hair around his fingers.

I prop myself up on my elbow so I can get a good look at Nate's face. It's gorgeous as always, and he's smiling at me like I'm as bright as the sun. "How long did you want me to stay?"

"Forever," he says, shrugging like it's no big deal.

I smile.

Forever is such a beautiful word.

Chapter
TWENTY-ONE

"I really like these pants," I say, tugging on the waistband. My finger brushes against the sewn-on logo that I designed; looking at it still gives me chills. "I think they could be a go for the women's line."

"I'll tell the R and D guys," Nate says as he sits down behind me, spreading his legs to make a spot for me.

"R and D guys," I say, parroting him. "I still can't believe this is happening. You, an *entrepreneur*." I say the last word with a fake French flourish that makes Nate laugh.

"I'm a small business owner." Nate keeps saying that, but it's not really true. Small business owners don't typically have the connections he does from his years in the sporting goods industry. Small business owners don't usually have the number of preorders that Rocky Mountain Rec does before they've even started production. But that title makes him feel safe, so I let him have it.

I pull my hair back into a ponytail as I look out on the valley below me. The lake is so still that it looks like a mirror for the sky.

"I just climbed a mountain, Nate. A *mountain*."

His laugh is a low rumble as he reaches forward and slides his calloused hands up and down my calves. We've been together a year, and I still shiver at even the slightest bit of contact. "It's a hill, Cal. Like…a really big hill."

"Hills have grass," I protest, turning to look at him. "This is definitely a rocky surface."

"Okay. It's a big, rocky hill."

I glare at him, but he grins and all my (mostly) fake outrage melts away.

"I'm standing on the precipice of…something!" I shout, shaking my fist triumphantly.

"If you're standing on anything, it's a slope."

I swat at his arms until his hands fall away. "Really? I'm supposed to be committing myself to you for life a week from tomorrow, and this is how you're playing the last dark days of your wifeless existence? By antagonizing your long-suffering fiancée?"

He plays so dirty, tickling the backs of my knees until I collapse in a fit of giggles. He takes advantage of my weakened state and gathers me in his arms, until I'm situated between his legs, one of my favorite spots.

"As if you could resist marrying this," he teases as our fingers tangle together.

"I'm not sure you're as much of a prize as you think you are," I say, lying through my teeth. I know how very lucky I am.

"You love me," he whispers, pressing his lips against my neck.

"I do," I tell him. "I do."

Love is the only word I can assign to all the feelings I have for him, even though I know that what we have goes much, much deeper than that.

"We should've asked for presents," he says, leaning forward so that his chin is resting on the top of my head. "Registered or whatever." He absently plays with my engagement ring, which is a thing he likes to do sometimes. He just turns it around and around my finger as he holds my hand, like he needs a tangible reminder that I'm here, we're real, and soon we'll be forever. I wonder if I'll do something similar with his ring once he's wearing it. I'm excited to find out; it seems like it's been sitting in my sock drawer for a lifetime, just waiting to be placed on his finger.

I only have to wait one more week. An eternity.

"We did ask for a present," I remind him. "Our honeymoon, if that rings a bell. And you'll be glad we asked for donations once you see the view from our hotel in the Alps."

He plants a soft kiss to the sensitive spot just below my ear. "We'll need a good view since I don't think we'll be going outside all that often."

The undercurrent of anticipation in his voice makes me feel like a thousand butterflies were set loose in my stomach. "We're getting married," I whisper.

"I can't wait."

I can't believe how far I've come over the past year. The ease with which Nate and I settled into a life together still surprises me, not that it should. Loving him was like breathing once I finally let myself do it. "I never would've thought that trip to Virginia would've led to all this," I admit.

Nate's fingers tighten around mine and he pulls me a little bit closer.

"So, what you're saying is that Ben and Gabby's wedding was the best thing that ever happened to you?"

I know he's teasing me, but what he said is true. Well, kind of.

"Nah," I tell him. "The greatest thing that ever happened to me had already happened by the time I got there."

"What's that?" he asks, gently cupping my cheek and turning my head until our eyes meet.

He already knows the answer, he just wants to hear me say it. I kiss him before I do.

"Meeting Mister Wright."

About the Author

CASSIE CROSS

Visit my website for the latest news and upcoming releases:
www.cassiecross.com

Follow me on Twitter: CrossWrites

Cassie Cross is a Maryland native and a romantic at heart, who lives outside of Baltimore with her two dogs and a closet full of shoes. Cassie's fondness for swoon-worthy men and strong women are the inspiration for most of her stories, and when she's not busy writing a book, you'll probably find her eating takeout and indulging in her love of 80's sitcoms.

Look for the following upcoming titles:

**The Billionaire's Desire #6: The Billionaire's Wedding -
Available April 2014**

The Billionaire's Best Friend - Coming Soon

Love You Madly - Summer 2014

Currently available titles:

The Billionaire's Desire #1: The Billionaire's Assistant
The Billionaire's Desire #2: The Billionaire's Seduction
The Billionaire's Desire #3: The Billionaire's Secret
The Billionaire's Desire #4: The Billionaire's Betrayal
The Billionaire's Desire #5: The Billionaire's Heart

This paperback interior was designed and formatted by

www.emtippettsbookdesigns.blogspot.com

Artisan interiors for discerning authors and publishers.

Printed in Poland
by Amazon Fulfillment
Poland Sp. z o.o., Wrocław